I0811309

Current Controversies

The Business of College Sports

Who Earns What

Other Books in the Current Controversies Series

America's Role in a Changing World
Artificial Intelligence and the Future of Humanity
Big Tech and Democracy
The Capitol Riot: Fragile Democracy
Climate Change and Biodiversity
Cyberterrorism
Domestic Extremism
Media Trustworthiness
The Politics and Science of COVID-19
Reparations for Black Americans
Space: Tourism, Competition, Militarization

Current Controversies

The Business of College Sports

Who Earns What

Gary Wiener, Book Editor

GREENHAVEN PUBLISHING

Published in 2023 by Greenhaven Publishing, LLC
29 E. 21st Street
New York, NY 10010

First Edition

Articles in Greenhaven Publishing anthologies are often edited for length to meet page requirements. In addition, original titles of these works are changed to clearly present the main thesis and to explicitly indicate the author's opinion. Every effort is made to ensure that Greenhaven Publishing accurately reflects the original intent of the authors. Every effort has been made to trace the owners of the copyrighted material.

Cover image: Jamie Lamor Thompson/Shutterstock.com

Library of Congress Cataloging-in-Publication Data

Names: Wiener, Gary, editor of compilation.
Title: The business of college sports : who earns what / Gary Wiener, book editor.
Description: First Edition. | New York : Greenhaven Publishing, 2023. | Series: Current Controversies | Includes bibliographical references and index. | Audience: Ages 15+ years | Audience: Grades 10–12 | Summary: "Anthology of essays exploring athletes and athletic programs at the university level"— Provided by publisher.
Identifiers: LCCN 2021062265 | ISBN 9781534508927 (Library Binding) | ISBN 9781534508910 (Paperback) | ISBN 9781534508934 (eBook)
Subjects: LCSH: College sports—Economic aspects—United States—Juvenile literature. | College athletes—United States—Juvenile literature. | National Collegiate Athletic Association—Juvenile literature.
Classification: LCC GV351 .B87 2023 | DDC 796.04/30973—dc23/eng/20220223
LC record available at https://lccn.loc.gov/2021062265

Manufactured in the United States of America

Website: http://greenhavenpublishing.com

Contents

Foreword

Controversy" is a word that has an undeniably unpleasant connotation. It carries a definite negative charge. Controversy can spoil family gatherings, spread a chill around classroom and campus discussion, inflame public discourse, open raw civic wounds, and lead to the ouster of public officials. We often feel that controversy is almost akin to bad manners, a rude and shocking eruption of that which must not be spoken or thought of in polite, tightly guarded society. To avoid controversy, to quell controversy, is often seen as a public good, a victory for etiquette, perhaps even a moral or ethical imperative.

Yet the studious, deliberate avoidance of controversy is also a whitewashing, a denial, a death threat to democracy. It is a false sterilizing and sanitizing and superficial ordering of the messy, ragged, chaotic, at times ugly processes by which a healthy democracy identifies and confronts challenges, engages in passionate debate about appropriate approaches and solutions, and arrives at something like a consensus and a broadly accepted and supported way forward. Controversy is the megaphone, the speaker's corner, the public square through which the citizenry finds and uses its voice. Controversy is the life's blood of our democracy and absolutely essential to the vibrant health of our society.

Our present age is certainly no stranger to controversy. We are consumed by fierce debates about technology, privacy, political correctness, poverty, violence, crime and policing, guns, immigration, civil and human rights, terrorism, militarism, environmental protection, and gender and racial equality. Loudly competing voices are raised every day, shouting opposing opinions, putting forth competing agendas, and summoning starkly different visions of a utopian or dystopian future. Often these voices attempt to shout the others down; there is precious little listening and considering among the cacophonous din. Yet listening and considering, too, are essential to the health of a democracy. If controversy is democracy's lusty lifeblood, respectful listening and careful thought are its higher faculties, its brain, its conscience.

Current Controversies does not shy away from or attempt to hush the loudly competing voices. It seeks to provide readers with as wide and representative as possible a range of articulate voices on any given controversy of the day, separates each one out to allow it to be heard clearly and fairly, and encourages careful listening to each of these well-crafted, thoughtfully expressed opinions, supplied by some of today's leading academics, thinkers, analysts, politicians, policy makers, economists, activists, change agents, and advocates. Only after listening to a wide range of opinions on an issue, evaluating the strengths and weaknesses of each argument, assessing how well the facts and available evidence mesh with the stated opinions and conclusions, and thoughtfully and critically examining one's own beliefs and conscience can the reader begin to arrive at his or her own conclusions and articulate his or her own stance on the spotlighted controversy.

This process is facilitated and supported in each Current Controversies volume by an introduction and chapter overviews that provide readers with the essential context they need to begin engaging with the spotlighted controversies, with the debates surrounding them, and with their own perhaps shifting or nascent opinions on them. Chapters are organized around several key questions that are answered with diverse opinions representing all points on the political spectrum. In its content, organization, and methodology, readers are encouraged to determine the authors' point of view and purpose, interrogate and analyze the various arguments and their rhetoric and structure, evaluate the arguments' strengths and weaknesses, test their claims against available facts and evidence, judge the validity of the reasoning, and bring into clearer, sharper focus the reader's own beliefs and conclusions and how they may differ from or align with those in the collection or those of classmates.

Research has shown that reading comprehension skills improve dramatically when students are provided with compelling, intriguing, and relevant "discussable" texts. The subject matter of these collections could not be more compelling, intriguing, or urgently relevant to today's students and the world they are poised to inherit. The anthologized articles also provide the basis for stimulating, lively, and passionate classroom debates. Students who are compelled to anticipate objections to their own argument and identify the flaws in those of an opponent read more carefully, think more critically, and steep themselves in relevant context, facts, and information more thoroughly. In short, using discussable text of the kind provided by every single volume in the Current Controversies series encourages close reading, facilitates reading comprehension, fosters research, strengthens critical thinking, and greatly enlivens and energizes classroom discussion and participation. The entire learning process is deepened, extended, and strengthened.

If we are to foster a knowledgeable, responsible, active, and engaged citizenry, we must provide readers with the intellectual, interpretive, and critical-thinking tools and experience necessary to make sense of the world around them and of the all-important debates and arguments that inform it. We must encourage them not to run away from or attempt to quell controversy but to embrace it in a responsible, conscientious, and thoughtful way, to sharpen and strengthen their own informed opinions by listening to and critically analyzing those of others. This series encourages respectful engagement with and analysis of current controversies and competing opinions and fosters a resulting increase in the strength and rigor of one's own opinions and stances. As such, it helps readers assume their rightful place in the public square and provides them with the skills necessary to uphold their awesome responsibility—guaranteeing the continued and future health of a vital, vibrant, and free democracy.

Introduction

> *"Nowhere else in America can businesses get away with agreeing not to pay their workers a fair market rate on the theory that their product is defined by not paying their workers a fair market rate. And under ordinary principles of antitrust law, it is not evident why college sports should be any different."*
>
> *—Justice Brett Kavanaugh*[1]

In early November 2021, Michigan State University's football team was in the middle of a banner year, boasting an 8-1 record, including a victory over arch-rival University of Michigan. The university rewarded head coach Mel Tucker by reportedly offering him a ten-year, $95 million contract. The following week, Tucker's team was beaten by Ohio State 56-7. The Twitterverse came out in full force. "Tucker must have been counting his money instead of preparing the team," one wrote. Another indulged in a bit of hyperbole: "So Mel Tucker signed a $100 million contract right before losing by 100 to Ohio State. Bold strategy."

Yet Tucker still had strong supporters. One stated, "Mel Tucker is a phenomenal leader, our team could have folded after a 49-0 halftime deficit but instead you saw guys continue to fight and battle for the last 30 minutes. It may not seem like a lot but that shows the type of culture being built in East Lansing."

In the ever-changing and lucrative world of major college sports, $95 million is the new threshold for what it costs to secure a coach at an elite football program. Soon after Tucker's contract became known, Notre Dame head coach Brian Kelly received a similar offer from the Southeastern Conference's Louisiana State University. With inflation running high in the 2020s, these figures are likely to keep growing.

Such exorbitant spending has flourished because coaches are the rock stars of collegiate sports. Though no coach has ever scored a touchdown, kicked a field goal, or slam dunked a basketball, at the college level the best athletes come and go, sometimes in as little as one year, to professional sports. At most, a college athlete can play for four years. But coaches are the face of the program. Successful ones, such as Duke basketball's Mike Krzyzewski or Alabama football's Nick Saban, may run one program for decades. Proponents of paying coaches high salaries argue that building a successful program doesn't come cheaply. Opponents insist that it is the athletes who do all the real work and deserve the compensation.

Until recently, college athlete compensation was highly restricted. While it is true that top student-athletes were offered scholarships that paid sometimes in excess of fifty or sixty thousand dollars a year, many of the best athletes did not stay in school long enough to take advantage of this perk by obtaining a degree. "Nothing about college athletics suggests that being a student comes first," says Danté Stewart, a former Clemson football player. But the NCAA, in order to promote the myth that college players were young scholars first and foremost so that they could avoid sharing their profits with the athletes, concocted the term "student-athlete." As Walter Byers, executive director of the NCAA from 1951–1987 explained in his memoir: "We crafted the term student-athlete and soon it was embedded in all NCAA rules and interpretations as a mandated substitute for such words as players and athletes."

But in 2021, in *NCAA v. Alston*, the Supreme Court ruled that barring athletes from benefiting from their own exploits was unjust. Justice Brett Kavanaugh took issue with the NCAA's notion of amateurism that traditionally prevented student-athletes from making money. According to Kavanaugh, the NCAA model suppressed "the pay of student athletes who collectively generate billions of dollars in revenues for colleges every year." Kavanaugh added, "Those enormous sums of money flow to seemingly everyone except the student athletes. College presidents, athletic directors, coaches, conference commissioners, and NCAA executives take in six- and seven-figure salaries. Colleges build lavish new facilities. But the student athletes who generate the revenues, many of whom are African American and from lower-income backgrounds, end up with little or nothing." Kavanaugh's words were all the more powerful in that they came from a notoriously conservative, pro-business judge.

And so, in light of the Supreme Court decision, "Name, Image, and Likeness" (NIL) rules were enacted that allowed college athletes to monetize their athletic prowess. For top players, the payoffs can be substantial. Alabama head football coach Nick Saban estimated that his star quarterback, Bryce Young, had signed deals worth nearly $1 million before the 2021 season had even begun. With over 5 million social media followers, high school basketball star Mikey Williams inked a contract with Excel Sports Management that will reportedly earn him millions. Entertainment lawyer Roy Maughan Jr. estimates that LSU gymnast Olivia Dunne could strike a deal worth $4 to $5 million. UConn basketball sensation Paige Bueckers signed a lucrative, multi-year deal with StockX, a footwear and apparel marketplace platform.

These contracts are the outliers. What NIL will mean for the average collegiate athlete remains to be seen, though early estimates range in the thousands of dollars.

Undeniably, the business of college sports is changing rapidly in the twenty-first century. Collegiate basketball, football, and even baseball (as well as hockey, volleyball, and other "lesser" sports) are growing more popular, attracting a more ardent fan base, gaining more television airtime, and, consequently, pulling in more money. The outsized enthusiasm that college football engenders was clearly on view in late November 2021 when, for the first time in a decade, the University of Michigan football team defeated its great rival, Ohio State University. Despite COVID-19 protocols, 100,000 elated Michigan fans swarmed onto the field after the game. One might have thought the United States had just won World War II for all the joy that these fans displayed. The state of Michigan was a happier place in the days that followed.

Major college sports can have that effect on its fans. All of the importance placed on collegiate sports programs raises several pertinent questions. Should colleges even be in the sports entertainment business? Is college sports really worth throwing this type of money at? Who benefits the most from college sports, the players or the adults? Though players are now allowed to reap rewards from their own name, image, and likeness, are they still pawns in a high-stakes game being played by those who supervise them? These are some of the many questions that the viewpoints in *Current Controversies: The Business of College Sports* tackle.

Notes

1. *NCAA v. Alston*, 594 U.S. (2021) (Kavanaugh B. concurring opinion).

Current Controversies

CHAPTER 1

Should Colleges and Universities Be in the Sports Business?

Overview: A Review of the NCAA's Business Model

Joshua A. Senne

Joshua A. Senne is a doctoral student at the United States Sports Academy with an emphasis in sports fitness and health and a specialization in sports marketing. He holds a master of business administration from Frostburg State University and a master of science in recreation and sport management from Indiana State University.

It's no secret that the National Collegiate Athletic Association (NCAA) has always been under fire for the way that it governs the institutions and players that participate in its events. Many would argue that the NCAA exploits the student-athletes through stringent rules and regulations that only allow the athlete to receive a certain, limited financial benefit in the form of scholarships, prevents the ability to play professional sports, except under very specific conditions, and also doesn't allow the institution to give the athletes any additional funding. Also, the student is not allowed to earn money as an athlete while a player under the NCAA's governing structure. The NCAA would argue the need for amateurism and the importance of stressing the educational focus on the way in which it governs the participating institutions, but there is big money in college sports, and very little actually goes to the ones responsible for generating that revenue, the student-athletes.

There is the point of view that the institutions are making big money within the NCAA, but realistically, most of them are at a loss of revenue. The Division I level institutions that win the big tournaments and games are the ones who reap the most benefit, and are most likely to have a positive net profit

"A Review of the NCAA's Business Model, Amateurism, and Paying the Players," by Joshua Senne, United States Sports Academy. Reprinted by permission.

at the end of the fiscal year. It's also not easy to reform the NCAA's regulations without running into some legal issues. This paper presents an overview of the following topics: (1) the NCAA as an organization and its purpose, (2) how the NCAA generates revenue and distributes this revenue to participating institutions, (3) the amateurism model of the NCAA and its reason for existing, (4) policy formation and adoption in relation to pay-for-play, and (5) key issues and problems that result from the current amateurism regulations, in addition to the problem with considering any proposal allowing for athletes to receive remuneration.

Review of the Literature

NCAA as an Organization

The NCAA is a member-led organization dedicated to the well-being and lifelong success of college athletes.[18] Further, it is a non-profit association, which regulates athletes of 1,281 institutions, conferences, organizations, and individuals, and it also organizes the athletic programs of many colleges and universities in the United States and Canada, and helps over 450,000 student-athletes who compete annually in college sports.[11, 1] The organization itself is located in Indianapolis, Indiana. The NCAA is considered to be the dominant organization governing college sports today in the United States, and while there are other organizations like the National Association of Intercollegiate Athletics (NAIA), the NCAA has been the most prominent.[15]

One of the key distinctions between the collegiate athletics and professional athletics is the role of profit, and college sports are focused on more than just profit. Collegiate athletics focuses on interests such as student morale, campus public relations, institutional profile, fundraising, and student physical fitness.[15] A misconception many often have about the NCAA when thinking about collegiate sports, is the governing structure of the organization. Essentially, it is not a large organization that dictates what occurs in the governance of collegiate sports, but rather the NCAA is governed by its over 1,200 member institutions.

The NCAA is divided into three divisions, which consist of Division I, II, and III. In 2008-2009, 330 institutions were competing in the Division I subdivisions: 119 in the Football Bowl Subdivision, 118 in the Football Championship Subdivision, and 93 in the Division I without Football Subdivision.[15] The Division II level had 282 institutions, and Division III had 422 institutions. It is these institutions that decide how collegiate sports will operate via the numerous representative paths in the NCAA. Further, governing rules range from eligibility to the operation of championships, and the rules and regulations of the NCAA are set forth in the organization's constitution and bylaws, which are available in the NCAA Manual.[15]

NCAA Revenue Generation and Distribution

As previously stated, the NCAA divides colleges and universities into three divisions according to the depth of their financial commitment. The top group is Division I, which is subdivided into I-A and II-A for football, and then there is Division II and III, which are low-cost activities.[13] The primary asset of the NCAA is the Division I men's basketball tournament, with a budget of $661 million in the 2008-2009 season, and nearly 90% of this was generated by the NCAA's previous 11-year, $6.2 billion contract with CBS to broadcast what has become widely known as "March Madness."[15] The NCAA replaced the last 3 years of this deal with a 14-year, $10.8 billion contract with CBS and Turner through 2024, which will provide the NCAA with an average of $771 million per year.[15]

The NCAA cedes its marketing rights to CBS, which sells the sponsorships, and top-level NCAA sponsors pay a reported $35 million annually, with second-tier sponsors paying $10-12 million annually. Further, another 6% was earned in ticket sales for the tournament.[15] The NCAA does not control the revenues associated with the Division I-A football post-season, even though the revenue potential seems to be much greater than that of basketball.

Individual conferences and schools negotiate separate broadcast agreements for regular-season football; a separate coalition of top conferences and Notre Dame control the post-season through the Bowl Championship Series (BCS), and all other post-season games are controlled by the promoters of the various independent bowl games that have entered into individual agreements with broadcast networks and cable channels.[15] The NCAA distributes the majority of its revenues to the members of Division I through various mechanisms, with these distributions totaling $387.2 million of the NCAA's expenses in 2008-2009. Further, another $49.9 million of the NCAA's revenues were distributed to the members of Divisions II and III as mandated by the NCAA constitution.[15]

Bergmann[2] would argue that the revenues received by colleges and universities seldom generate a profit, and often drains the institution of profits because of the amount of money being spent to build the best teams and win tournaments. Further, she argues that the need to win these NCAA tournaments puts a drain on non-athletic resources to support the athletic department's goals, and also that when the athletic department is profitable, it doesn't seem to support the academic side of the institution. There are many arguments that can be made towards the NCAA, but it would seem that the NCAA benefits the most by exploiting college institutions and athletes. Institutions can be profitable under the NCAA, but only when they are a winning team, and even then, depending on what division they are in and the expenditures by the athletic department, it may not be profitable.[8]

For the NCAA, institutions are capable of making profits from participating in the NCAA, but this is mostly if they are a winning team in the Division I area because this is where a lot of the revenue distribution is concerned. Also, institutions can make money by getting money from students through fees, athletic shops, and gate sales. The question for an institution is really about how much the school is spending on upgrading the athletic program, and whether or not profits from the athletic program outweigh expenditures.

Amateurism

According to Shropshire,[16] there is a common misperception that the foundation of collegiate amateurism had its origination in the Olympic model of the ancient Greeks. The "myth" of ancient amateurism held that there was some society, presumably the Greeks, that took part in a sport solely for the associated glory while receiving no compensation for either participating or winning.[16] However, it is argued that there is no mention of amateurism in Greek sources, and no reference to amateur athletes, and no reference that the term even existed in antiquity.[16] Further, it would appear that the myth was perpetuated by scholars who would apparently have a direct benefit from the implementation of such a system.

In 1866, the Amateur Athletic Club of England published a definition of the term "amateur," and although the term had been in use for many years, this may have potentially been the first official definition of the word.[16] Further, at this time, the idea of amateurism was that people who competed for money were of questionable character, and that those of the working class were not allowed to compete in amateur sports because the workers had an unfair advantage in that working helped them to develop muscles, giving them an unfair advantage. Further, it was idealized that if an amateur athlete were to lose to a laborer, he would lose his status in society. This led to the development of the "mechanics clause," which is the belief that the use of muscles as part of one's employment offered an unfair competitive advantage.[16] The NCAA essentially evolved from these antiquated rules of keeping amateur sports based on the ability and social position of an athlete, and not on money.

The issue, which confronts amateurism in the U.S. today, is based on the presumption that a college competes purely at an amateur level and will lose prestige and revenue as it loses contests.[16] Further, open acknowledgment of the adoption of professionalism would result in a loss of respectability for the university as a bastion for academia.[16] Therefore, the resolution to this dilemma has been for institutions to claim amateurism, but operate under a professional mode of operation. Initially, many institutions ignored the first eligibility code by the NCAA, which stated that students only need to be full-time and not paid for play. This caused the NCAA to further define its views of amateurism and implement the formal adoption of the Amateur Code in the NCAA constitution, which is to incorporate the definition and principles of the amateur spirit, and to "widen the scope of government."[16]

It can be stated that the NCAA sought to strengthen its governing power over amateurism by the slow integration and adoption of more rules and regulations. This has always been an issue within the NCAA, wherein people have sought to advocate change within in the Constitution and Bylaws, wherein athletes receive compensation beyond the weak scholarships they are given, in the form of stipends or pay-for-play.[15] Some would argue that most of the regulatory activity in the NCAA engages in is illegal.[6] For example, actions such as the establishment of limits on the type and amount of financial aid appear to be price-fixing. However, the Supreme Court has recognized that under certain circumstance, the NCAA is allowed to take such actions.[6]

So what is the reason for not paying the athletes? Wouldn't it make sense to pay them what they are worth, or even to the level of their marginal revenue product (MRP) within a similar model of the professional leagues? Well, the NCAA believes that amateur athletics are an integral part of the educational experience, and that professionalizing the programs would destroy this concept of the student-athlete.[6] Further, while some coaches would support the notion of paying their athletes, they state that they already struggle to profit from their current athletic programs under the current amateurism model, so paying the athletes would potentially further strain the athletics budget, especially if it's not profitable.[6] One could argue that many Division I schools can absorb the costs of paying athletes if it cut certain unnecessary costs on existing programs and on extravagance.

Policy Formation and Adoption

In the NCAA, the amateurism policy is Article 12 of the NCAA Division I Manual, and under Article 12 in Sub-article 12.2.5 Contracts and Compensation, it states that any individual is ineligible for participation in intercollegiate athletics if he or she has entered into an agreement to compete in professional sports either in writing or orally.[10] The exception to this rule is sub sub-article 12.2.5.1 Exception—Before Initial Fulltime Collegiate Enrollment—Sports Other Than Men's Ice Hockey and Skiing, which states that an individual may participate in professional sports other than men's ice hockey or skiing as long as the agreement was made before full-time collegiate enrollment and the individual is not paid for participation in excess of the cost to participate.[10]

Further, in sub sub-article 12.2.5.2 Nonbinding Agreement, if an individual signs a contract of commitment to a professional team that is not binding until a rep from the professional team signs it or an agent signs is also ineligible, even if they never sign the contract.[10] This policy of contracts and compensation under the amateurism policy can be considered a conditional form of policy because for an individual to be eligible, he or she must follow the conditions set forth by this policy on amateurism, which states that individuals may not participate in intercollegiate athletics unless certain conditions are met and followed. In this case, the condition is that an individual has not made any agreements to compete in professional athletics, and assuming that the exceptions stated are not relevant to the particular case.

The systems model of policy-making, developed by Easton, consists of 4 components, which take place in a structural, social, political, and economic environment. This environment affects all parts of the system. The first part of the system is the input, and the inputs to the policy-making system are the demands placed on the system to do something about a problem. With the inputs, the political system translates them into outputs, and the structural, social, political, and economic environments influence political and policy-making activities. The results of translating the inputs are the outputs, which consist of laws, regulations, and decisions. Key to the common definition of public policy as being what the government chooses to do or not to do is the idea of a decision. In policy making, someone or some institution in the policy process has to make a decision. The decisions are what laws to enact and regulations to apply to public and private programs. Based on the feedback received from these outputs, there will either be new inputs to translate, or the policy makers will choose to evaluate the program after overseeing it to make sure it is reaching its goals, and if it isn't, policy makers will make changes and make new outputs.

The stages model of policy making is very similar to the systems model, except that it is broken down into more parts. The Stages Model of policy-making is a step-by-step process of policy making, which starts at the beginning and ends at the end, unlike the systems model, which goes to inputs or policy makers. The stages of the stage model begin with issues emergence, then agenda setting, then alternative selection, enactment, implementation, and then evaluation. After evaluation, the process of the stages model loops back to the beginning to issue emergence. Like the systems model, there is an issue or input, which is translated (agenda setting and alternative selection), then outputted (enactment, implementation), and then evaluated (feedback). The difference is that instead of going back to the policy makers, it goes back to issue emergence.

Decision-making consists of a judgment, which is a choice between alternatives. Sport managers use their judgment to make a decision about whether to hire or fire employees, to add new programs, to sell off a division that is losing money, or trade a player. Decisions a manager makes can be divided into two categories, programmed and non-programmed decisions. Programmed decisions are repetitive and routine, and are made on the basis of clearly defined policies and procedures and a manager's past experience. Non-programmed decisions are new and unique, which have no established guidelines or procedures as to the way these decisions should be made.

One model of decision-making, which will be used to compare to policy-making models is the rational model. The Rational Model is a linear step-by-step analysis of the problem situation and the identification of solutions. This is a model of the way decisions should be made and not necessarily the way they are made. The first stage of the rational model consists of monitoring the decision environment, which is when the sport manager is scanning an organization for deviations from the expected norm. Next, the problem is defined about which a decision is needed to be made, the problem is diagnosed, alternatives are identified, the alternatives are analyzed, the best alternatives are selected, then implemented, and then the decisions are evaluated.

The difference between decision-making and policy making are that in decision-making the sport manager looks for problems with which to identify and then addresses the problem according through a process much like the stages model of policy making. Also, much like the stages model of policy making, the decisions are implemented, then evaluated. Another difference between policy-making and rational decision-making process is that in the rational model, managers are likely to neglect the outcome of decisions because they don't like to find that they made a wrong decision.[3]

An example of policy-making in sport management is when UCONN's Shabazz Napier recently told reporters he sometimes goes to bed "starving" because he can't afford food, despite that UCONN's student-athlete guidelines include provisions for meal plans.[5] After this incident, Rep. Matthew Lesser said he and other state lawmakers are considering legislation.[5] Further, Napier added that he's going to bed hungry when millions of dollars are being made off of him.[5] Lesser stated that it was a problem with the NCAA because he wanted to make sure he was putting pressure on them.[5] Due to the pressure the NCAA was receiving because of the statements made by Napier, the NCAA legislative council wasted no time in changing the meal plan policy from 3 meals a day to unlimited.[17] This is an example of policy making in sports management in which there was an input, which was translated, and then an output. The input was the issue of athletes starving, the translation was the NCAA Legislative Council's probing of the issue, and the output was their decision to change the then current policy.

Key Issues with Pay-for-Play

For quite a while, there has been an issue with the NCAA and the perception that it is making a lot of money off of student-athletes, but only giving out nominal distributions in return for the profits made off of them. Further, the symptoms of the issue seem to be exacerbated by the fact that the NCAA creates strict guidelines in regards to the way the student-athlete is governed while on an amateur sports team within the NCAA. The pay-for-play advocates in collegiate sports seem to be under the impression that athletes who demonstrate success to an institution are entitled to revenue for their efforts.[4] The understanding of the NCAA and other adversaries of the pay-for-play realized this notion would restructure the mission statement of the student-athlete and threaten what college athletics is all about, education.[4]

According to Forik,[4] a common misconception found in research was that athletic departments generate a substantial amount of money as departments were often times operating at a loss, and educating advocates would ultimately help them comprehend that this was an inadequate, unattainable proposal and would eradicate the majority, if not all, collegiate sports.[4] Essentially, to move forward with this concept would bring liability issues and contribute further to the already decreasing economic concerns of athletic departments.[4] There have been proposals presented by different scholars and sport management professionals to the NCAA, which offer some different perspectives and ideas for giving college athletes some sort of remuneration for their services as an athlete.

Goplerud[6] presents one such proposal wherein he states the NCAA should develop legislation providing for stipends for athletes in major revenue-producing sports at the Division I level, and the stipends should be made available to men in football and basketball and women in basketball, volleyball, and other sports in sufficient numbers to satisfy gender requirements. The exact amount of the stipend to the individual athlete would be within the discretion of the individual school, and the student-athletes would have a salary cap of $300 a month per scholarship athlete, with half of the money going into a trust fund to be paid to those athletes receiving degrees within five years of matriculation. Some other aspects of this proposal would be that student-athletes could work during the semester and would not have a cap on their earnings. Also, the school could decide to pay less than the cap or not pay a stipend at all to the student-athletes.

Some issues with accepting a proposal such as the one aforementioned, are worker's compensation, gender equity, labor law, and taxation issues. If a proposal like this were to be adopted, then it is probable that in most jurisdictions the athletes receiving stipends would then be covered by the workers compensation laws of those states, and coverage brings with it legal and financial considerations for the athletic departments impacted.[6, 4] Further, when considering gender equity, schools providing stipends under the proposal would have to provide the stipends for a proportionate number or women athletes, and any disparities would cause legal issues and subject the school to sanctions under law.[6]

Another issue arising from a stipend proposal is the question of whether the athletes would be considered employees of the National Labor Relations Act, and if the court were to approve this notion, then a whole host of major problems could face the NCAA's amateurism model. Lastly, there is the issue of taxation in relation to a proposal to allow for student-athletes to receive stipends. Currently, athletic scholarships are not taxable to the athlete, and if the stipend were added, then it is probable that at least a portion of the scholarship would constitute taxable income to the student-athlete.[5] This would further add the burden of withholding for income tax as well as social security and Medicare, and it might further provide fuel for those who advocate the general removal of tax-exempt status of collegiate athletics.

As one can see, allowing for student-athletes to get pay-for-play would threaten the amateurism model of the NCAA, but also create a whole host of other legal issues for the NCAA as well as the institution. Some would argue that the loss of collegiate sports in relation to amateurism wouldn't matter because of the money generated to the institutions and the effects of paying the players would outweigh the "benefits" given by the NCAA. In other words, if an athlete is being paid what they are worth, does it really matter if the institution is considered a supporter of amateurism? Goplerud[6] suggests that amateurism is not the reason most fans watch collegiate sports, but that loyalties to educational institutions and to tradition are very important.

With all of the aforementioned data, one could presumably argue the NCAA acts as nothing more than an intermediary between institutions, wherein it controls the distribution of funds to institutions and also to the athletes, while restricting the athlete's ability to make money from outside sources.[9, 14, 7] This is arguably exploitation of student-athletes, where in previously mentioned instances, student-athletes are not even able to feed themselves at night due to the lack of financial support from institutions due to NCAA restrictions. Further, if a coach attempts to pay the athletes by some other means, he or she can be fined.[12]

Essentially, one could argue that the NCAA should not have the power to influence the governance of collegiate athletics, and especially the athletes' ability to make money from outside sources during their tenure as student-athlete. This is exploitation and unethical, and while the notion of given importance to the value of education is a good gesture and also the mission and meaning of the NCAA, it would appear that it is worried a lot more about keeping the student-athlete focused on "school," but more importantly, on playing college sports, so that it has a profitable player to make money off of through broadcast rights.

Summary

It was discussed how the NCAA is a non-profit governing body of collegiate athletics throughout the United States and Canada. Its primary focus is to maintain the focus of collegiate athletics on giving student-athletes an opportunity to receive an education while also developing as an athlete. The NCAA is considered to be the dominant collegiate sports governing body, and it is divided into three divisions which consist of Divisions I, II, and III. Many believe that the NCAA governs what happens within collegiate sports, but the truth is the member institutions deliberate on how collegiate sports will operate, and this is done through various representative paths. Lastly, the scope of the NCAA range from regulating rules of eligibility to the operation of championships, and these rules and regulations can be found with the NCAA Manual.

While the NCAA is a non-profit organization, it generates quite a substantial revenue through contracts with CBS in the millions of dollars annually to cede its marketing rights. These revenues are split between institutions in scholarships and revenue distribution, but the revenue distribution is greater for those institutions that are in the top level of Division I athletics. It is mainly the winning teams that truly benefit from the revenue distribution of the NCAA because these winning teams receive a greater piece of the pie. Many think that institutions generate a lot of profit through collegiate athletics, but the truth is that many institutions athletics departments fail to generate a profit, and this is because so much money goes towards developing a winning team. That being said, one has to wonder how that affects the focus of education when educational funding suffers from athletic spending in many cases.

It seems as though the NCAA is exploiting is players through the notion of amateurism. While amateurism has been around for quite a long time, the notion that amateurism maintains the educational foundation within college athletics seems to be losing ground. The NCAA is focused on education as it states, but when athletes are struggling to survive, and in some cases, going to bed starving, one has to wonder how focused the NCAA truly is on the student and his or her education. With all of the money generated through the college athletes in the performance of their respective sport, it would make sense that these athletes would receive all necessary funding for attending college, not just college tuition. Further, to restrict the rights of athletes to play professional sports (except under certain conditions) or to profit from their athletic position seems rather unethical, especially since the NCAA and the institution stand to benefit from the performance of the college athlete.

The pay-for-subject is not likely to ever go away in regards to the NCAA and how it supports its student-athletes. It is likely that amateurism would either disappear altogether, or funding for the athletes would have to be pulled from somewhere else, and with a lot of athletic programs at institutions operating at a loss due to the overwhelming financial strain of trying to win tournaments, it is not likely to come from the institution. Further, the NCAA claims that the majority of its revenue generated is given back to schools in the form of scholarships, other programs, and also through revenue distribution to participating institutions that win games. That being said, if an institution isn't in the Division I level, and also doesn't win, the benefit of being a part of the NCAA is very little if any. Realistically, the NCAA stands to profit more from the control and oppression of its student-athletes through stringent regulations and rules. If the NCAA doesn't find a way to deliver a better benefit to the student-athlete while also incorporating the importance of education, it is likely to continue facing ethical, moral, and legal issues.

Recommendation

A great deal of research has been conducted and review articles have been written to investigate the pay-for-play topic, and also to investigate the perceived benefits of being a student-athlete at an institution that participates within the NCAA governing structure. Further research could look into the more detailed financial breakdown of the benefit of participating in the NCAA as an institution versus the cost of trying to win games as a member institution in the NCAA. One may find that it is not so profitable to participate in the NCAA and actually causes an institution to lose money. There are certain review articles that mention this topic, but no research in a detailed financial breakdown amongst institutions to evaluate the benefit versus the cost in a quantitative and qualitative fashion.

Recommendations for the NCAA are to seriously consider either allowing institutions to pay the players at least as far as living expenses and perhaps spending money is concerned, and also it should look at increasing the scholarship benefit to student-athletes so that the institutions do not have to bear the financial burden. The NCAA is seen as a cartel and that is not the public image one wants to portray to the public when the public is one's greatest revenue generator, but it can be seriously argued that the NCAA has been around for so long and has such a stronghold on collegiate athletics, it is not likely that anyone could strongly influence or cause a major change in the amateurism structure of the NCAA. Furthermore, the NCAA needs to seriously consider allowing students to receive product or brand sponsorships much in the same way as professional athletes. The NCAA doesn't stand to lose any money from this, and as long as the student-athlete is doing well in school, he or she should be allowed to grow his or her career and benefit from the success resulting from being a stellar student-athlete.

Conclusion

From the discussion, one can see there are quite a few dilemmas present within the NCAA and how it exploits the student-athlete, but on the other hand, one could argue that the NCAA provides a situation wherein the student-athlete is able to participate in a higher level of sports while also receiving an education. The weakness in the latter argument is the fact that student-athletes are generally trained strenuously 12 months out of the year, generate revenue for not only the NCAA, but also the institution for which they are playing. That being said, one has to wonder of the pressure put on athletes to perform and the long training schedules are worth the little financial benefit (scholarships). The institution itself stands to do quite well if it can get a strong team on the court or in the field.

There are also other issues within the NCAA in regards to proposals for stipends or pay-for-play. That is the issue of worker's compensation, labor laws, gender equity, and also taxation. When one starts paying the players based on their success, they potentially become an employee, unless of course the money is given in the form of a scholarship, but if they are paid a salary, then one could successfully argue that the player becomes an employee. This would open up a whole host of other issues for the NCAA, and so it is quite reasonable for the NCAA to consider reforming the way it distributes funds, but also allows the player to reap the benefits of their own success. One such way is to allow players to be paid for sponsoring products or brands, and another way is through better scholarships for student-athletes, but especially student-athletes in top performing institutions. As long as the student-athlete is maintaining the grade, he or she should be allowed to have more benefits like those in the professional league, just without the salary from the school or NCAA.

References

1. Amateurism and the future of the NCAA. (2013). Mississippi Sports Law Review, 3(1), 1-46.
2. Bergmann, B. R. (1991). Do sports really make money for the university? Academe, 77(1), 28-30. Retrieved from http://www.jstor.org/stable/40251010
3. Birkland, T. A. (2005). An introduction to the policy process: Theories, concepts, and models of public policy making (2nd ed.) (pp. 200-232). New York: M. E. Sharpe.
4. Forik, B. K. (2015). Assessing the economic concerns of the pay-for-play issue in collegiate sports. KAHPERD Journal, 28-31.
5. Ganim, S. (2014). UConn guard on unions: I go to bed “starving.” CNN U.S. Retrieved from http://www.cnn.com/2014/04/07/us/ncaa-basketball-finals-shabazz-napier-hungry/
6. Goplerud III, P. (2011). Symposium: Sports law as a reflection of society’s laws and values: Pay for play for college athletes: Now, more than ever. In S. Rosner & K. L. Shropshire, The business of sports (pp. 652-658). Sudbury, MA: Jones & Bartlett.
7. Lodge, A. (2016). Who’s afraid of the big bad NCAA?…The Ed O’Bannon v. NCAA decision’s impact on the NCAA’s amateurism model. Journal of Corporation Law, 41(3), 775-793.
8. Mangrum, B. (2014). Is college football profitable for universities? Ethos. Retrieved from http://www.ethosreview.org/intellectual-spaces/is-college-football-profitable/
9. McMillen, C. T. (2011). Eliminate the profit motive. Chronicle of Higher Education, A6.
10. National Collegiate Athletic Association. (2013). NCAA Division I Manual. Indianapolis, IN: NCAA.

11. National Collegiate Athletic Association. (2016). In Wikipedia, The Free Encyclopedia. Retrieved from https://en.wikipedia.org/w/index.php?title=National_Collegiate_Athletic_Association&oldid=741803145

12. NCAA sanctions Alaska-Anchorage coach for paying players. (2014). Journal of NCAA Compliance, 12.

13. Noll, R. C. (2011). The business of college sports and the high cost of winning. In S. Rosner & K. L. Shropshire, The business of sports (pp. 507-519). Sudbury, MA: Jones & Bartlett.

14. Paule, A. L., & Gilson, T. A. (2010). Current collegiate experiences of big-time, non-revenue, NCAA athletes. Journal of Intercollegiate Sport, 3(2), 333-347.

15. Rosner, S. R., & Shropshire, K. L. (2011). The business of sports. Sudbury, MA: Jones & Bartlett.

16. Shropshire, K. L. (2011). Legislation for the glory of sport: Amateurism and compensation. In S. Rosner & K. L. Shropshire, The business of sports (pp. 648-652). Sudbury, MA: Jones & Bartlett.

17. USA Today Sports. (2014). NCAA council votes to give student-athletes unlimited meals, snacks. USA TODAY. Retrieved from http://www.usatoday.com/story/sports/college/2014/04/15/ncaa-legislative-council-meals-student-athletes/7750413/

18. What is the NCAA. (2016). NCAA.org. Retrieved from http://www.ncaa.org/about/resources/media-center/ncaa-101/what-ncaa

Athletic Directors Must Care About Their Student-Athletes' Welfare

Greg Santore

Greg Santore is principle and managing director of the Sports Leadership practice for the executive search firm Witt/Kieffer. He has worked extensively with colleges, universities, governing bodies, and nonprofit organizations to identify and place exceptional sports leaders.

College sports flex a lot of muscle today. From TV contracts to t-shirts, they play an important role in securing alumni and donor support, building school pride and unity, and raising the overall profile of institutions. Even at smaller institutions—without the TV deals or revenue-generating sports—there is often the perception that athletic directors have outsized importance and wield too much power.

In reality, whether in Division I, II, or III, ADs must respect their schools' academic interests, goals, and culture—and take a back seat to the president. "The outside world sometimes forgets that while the athletics department may be the most visible part of the university, its overall impact to the university's bottom line is minuscule," says Chris Del Conte, director of intercollegiate athletics at Texas Christian University. "Even at TCU, the athletics department makes up a tiny percentage of the overall university operating budget." Because sports at TCU represent a majority of the university's media exposure, it can sometimes seem like the tail is wagging the dog, he notes.

Del Conte was one of several college athletics leaders who provided insights to *Forbes* columnist Jason Belzer and me recently for a collaborative article, "How Do Athletic Directors and University Presidents Manage to Get Along?" We asked ADs to explore the relationship between these two high-profile campus positions.

"It's the job of the athletic director to adjust his values and cultural expectations to that of the president, not the other way around," notes Peter Pilling, director of athletics at Columbia University.

These adjustments are easier when an athletic director's fluency with stats includes GPAs, not just Ws and Ls. As an executive recruiter, I come across many up-and-coming athletics administrators who have a sports-first, education-second mentality. What's needed in top athletic directors, however, is a healthy appreciation for both.

Cultural Fit

Athletic directors must nurture mutual respect with academic leaders. As Lou Anna Simon, president of Michigan State University, suggests: athletics and academics create a "tightly interconnected ecosystem with common values . . . with athletics as the front porch of the university." Simon was one of four presidents to provide input for another related *Forbes* column, "The Priorities of University Presidents: Where Do College Athletics Fit In?"

Simon sees the need for a well calibrated balance between athletics and academics interests. "If you're consistent with your values and your culture, you're going to turn out OK," she says.

This balanced relationship begins when athletic directors work with their presidents to establish and maintain a strong mission for their department, built upon ethics and integrity. The ADs must care about their student-athletes' welfare as well as the school's core values and educational objectives.

As in sports, team chemistry matters in academia. The lack of a cultural fit can undo an athletic director who otherwise seems well-matched with the school's expectations. Someone who manages too aggressively to the bottom line can fumble the support of vocal stakeholders, including students and alumni, who see strictly-business decisions running counter to their school's traditions.

A Well-Rounded Mix of Abilities

With a well-rounded mix of department leadership qualities, athletic directors can withstand the harsh spotlight often thrown on them. These traits include fairness (respecting diverse student interests, especially those of underrepresented minorities), patience (in cultivating donors), and faithfulness (to school values).

Barry Alvarez, athletic director at the University of Wisconsin, is widely thought to embody those qualities. Alvarez, the former football coach, is kind of an old-school example of today's athletic director, a throwback to the days when ADs were almost always promoted from within, usually from the school's own coaching ranks. Who would appreciate our culture better than an insider?

An unfortunate truth is that academia generally is not highly focused on internal career development and succession planning. So in today's athletics departments, low- to mid-level administrators need to actively pursue challenging internal opportunities and initiatives. By raising their profile by taking on progressive, important responsibilities, sports administrators call attention to their zeal for student athletics and their schools. Those qualities are critical to successful athletic director careers.

And while internal athletic director candidates, with a firm grasp of their school's culture and mission sensitivities, can get a leg up on external candidates, it's also true that athletic directors can come from the outside and, increasingly, "non-traditional" backgrounds. Nonprofit associations and sports foundations are great training grounds for leaders who can handle business responsibilities with diplomacy. A few corporate CEOs have made this transition as well, with decidedly mixed results.

Chief Executive Qualities

Big or small, collegiate sports programs are businesses. Amid the passion of school spirit and rivalries are the dispassionate matters of money, and athletic directors need the skills to handle all that. Financial acumen and discipline—tempered by sensitivity to the school's academic mission as well as the fan base of each sport—are critical.

The CEO/AD analogy applies with one emphatic note: the CEO needs to bring an entrepreneurial spirit. Gilbert M. Gaul, in his book *Billion-Dollar Ball: A Journey through the Big-Money Culture of College Football*, takes a hard look at the business. He writes about the "new financial model" in which leadership expects athletic directors to find their own money rather than depend upon general revenues.

This model will force athletic directors to be savvy financial managers and creative fundraisers. There are wide revenue disparities among programs within schools (that is, basketball, football, and just about every other sport) and between schools (the top 25 moneymakers and everyone else). Dealing with these disparities to the satisfaction of student-athletes, coaches, and fans—and the school's mission—requires the strategic capability to make tough calls.

Meanwhile, the NCAA's ongoing reform efforts call for an understanding of the nuances of governance. Athletic directors need to stay on top of national issues such as student-athlete transfer rules and practice time limits, and factor those considerations into how they do business.

Winning hearts, minds, and dollars won't be easy for tomorrow's collegiate athletic directors. Their presidents are feeling pressures to control expenses and limit tuition hikes. And for state schools, public funding for higher education is uncertain. Competition for resources is only getting tougher.

Future ADs

Present and future athletic directors can help their cause if they look at the bigger picture of sports on campus today. Even with TCU's Del Conte's assertion that sports contribute a small percentage to a school's general budget, school presidents see the value. They made that point clear in their interview for *Forbes*.

"Winning is not our first priority," said Biddy Martin, president of Amherst College. "We care more about the added value athletics brings to the overall student experience."

"Investing in athletics often has a higher ROI than in other university programs," says Michael Shonrock, president of Lindenwood University. "Student-athletes on average have higher GPAs and graduation rates than the general student body. . . . Yes, athletic administrators are more revenue-driven, but their bottom line is to graduate student-athletes first and foremost, and so they will be held accountable for that above all else."

Not all athletic directors are held fully accountable for upholding academic interests, of course. However, given the increased scrutiny placed upon college athletics by the media, fans, alums, and other stakeholders, the most successful athletic directors will be those who truly understand and support their schools' academic values and cultures.

Team Sports Offer Social and Academic Benefits

Paige Maslen

Paige Maslen is the associate director of marketing, media, and public relations at Army and Navy Academy, a private military boarding school in San Diego County, California.

Team sports are about so much more than their physical benefits. This is especially so when group sports activities are incorporated into a young person's life. Studies have shown a direct correlation between physical activity and academic performance. A University of Kansas study looking at the performance of students in grades 9 to 12 showed that more than 97% of student athletes graduated high school, 10% higher than those students who had never participated in sports. Athletes were also shown to have better G.P.A. outcomes than non-athletes.

This might have to do with the increased cognitive ability that comes from playing sports. Physical activity naturally increases blood flow to the brain and activates endorphins, chemicals that are released when you exercise. Endorphins can impact your mood and work performance, meaning athletes may be more willing and capable of tackling that next big problem.

Team sports can also help with emotional development. Research published by the Canadian Fitness and Lifestyle Research Institute states that exercise can lead to a unique state of short-term relaxation. That relaxation can promote increased concentration, better memory, enhanced creativity, more effective problem solving, and an improved mood—all benefits that will extend into the classroom.

Team athletes are constantly working with a slate of other people, many of whom can become positive role models along

"The Social and Academic Benefits of Team Sports," by Paige Maslen, Edutopia (The George Lucas Educational Foundation), December 29, 2015. Reprinted by permission.

the way. Team sports foster mentorship between older players and younger players, coaches and athletes, and more. Coaches in particular can play an important role in a young athlete's life. Players who have positive sports mentors when they're young are also more likely to seek effective role models throughout their life.

Soft skills are personal attributes that allow people to build positive social relationships. Team sports are an excellent source of soft skills development, as they allow athletes to grow within a supportive environment. Here are just a few of the soft skills fostered through team sports:

Communication Skills

While it might not be as obvious as sitting down and discussing a group project, team sports take a lot of communication—both spoken and unspoken. Communication skills are key in maintaining a functioning sports team, whether it's listening to locker room pep talk, picking up on nonverbal cues given by other players, or expressing a thought during a post-game debrief.

As Jill Prudden said in her book *Coaching Girl's Basketball Successfully*, players are expected to express their concerns, hopes, and disappointments to their coaches and their teammates. She also encourages her players to seek feedback from coaches as well as their classroom teachers, as a result fostering communications skills that will help them succeed in their academic endeavors.

Decisive Action

Sports plays happen fast, and athletes develop the skills needed to make effective snap decisions. Whether it's a basketball player deciding to shoot or a soccer player realizing his best move is to pass to a teammate for the assist, athletes learn critical decision-making skills that will benefit them both during and after game time.

Any athlete who has played in a championship game knows the meaning of pressure. Sports create an environment where athletes learn to conquer their natural "fight or flight" instinct to make consistent and difficult decisions under high pressure situations. This ability to function under pressure translates to person who is better at making deadlines and working in stressful situations in the future.

Teamwork

This is an obvious one. Teamwork is all about collaborating with others to reach a common goal. The diverse pairing of personalities and scenarios will help your athlete become adaptable, persistent, and patient. Team sports also teach a sense of group and individual responsibility.

Being on a team with a dozen or more of your peers is an excellent way to recognize the individual talents each person brings to the table. As the Janssen Sports Leadership Center says, working with teammates teaches athletes important life skills such as to respect one another, act in unselfish ways, make good decisions on behalf of the team, and not cut corners.

Time Management

The time commitment required by athletes can be comparable to that of a full-time job. Think of all the different commitments an athlete needs to juggle: competitions, strength and conditioning, team meetings, sports physiotherapy—and these are just the sports-related obligations!

Necessity demands that athletes learn valuable time management skills, otherwise they would never be able to keep up with academics and sport. Effective time management planning is part of why a recent article published by Fast Company argues employers should consider hiring a former student athlete.

Team athletes know that every second counts, and this value of time will translate to their everyday life. As Shannon Miller, a member of the 1992 and 1996 United States Olympic women's gymnastics team told *Forbes*, she kept a schedule that was almost minute by minute when she was an athlete. This careful planning and precision helps athletes focus on reaching their goals sooner than non-athletes.

Build Self-Esteem and a Sense of Community

Team sports are said to bolster the five C's: competence, confidence, connections, character, and caring. At the heart of this is self-esteem—an increased sense of self as a result of better social interactions, stronger relationships, and higher academic performance.

Team sports provide athletes with a natural community. A report from True Sport says that youth who play sports have higher levels of social support, and that the sense of community created with teammates, coaches, and family members incubates the perfect setting for critical self-esteem development.

In the end, the opportunity to participate in team sports provides athletes with valuable skills that will take them beyond the field, pitch, and court.

Being a Scholar-Athlete Offers Immense Rewards

Joseph L. Cross and Bruce W. Fouke

Joseph L. Cross is a postdoctoral fellow in outreach for the Carle R. Woese Institute for Genomic Biology at the University of Illinois at Urbana-Champaign. Bruce Fouke is a professor in geology and microbiology at the Carl R. Woese Institute for Genomic Biology at the University of Illinois at Urbana-Champaign.

According to the National Center for Education and Statistics, ~20.5 million students are projected to enroll in United States (U.S.) high schools in Fall 2017. Nearly eight million of these young people are formally involved in team sports (National Collegiate Athletic Association, 2018). These high school students will herein be referred to as Scholar-Athletes. In this context, the word "Scholar" refers to a student who develops a broad holistic approach to education that includes learning about everything from science and math to art and language. "Athlete" refers to students committed to achieving high performance and success in a wide variety of sports from basketball and soccer to fencing and archery. According to the document "NCAA Recruiting Facts," ~5–6 percent of the Scholar-Athletes who graduated from high school in 2017 will play NCAA collegiate sports (National Collegiate Athletic Association, 2018).

[...]

It is not easy for the scholar-athlete to fully commit to the dual role of scholar and athlete. It takes a person's full dedication for each of those roles. Talent is not only found in sports, but also comes in effective scheduling for classes, study time, work-outs, events, and rest (Axtell, 1991). This ability to

"Redefining the Scholar-Athlete," by Joseph LeAnthony Cross and Bruce W. Fouke, Frontiers Media S.A., August 16, 2019. https://www.frontiersin.org/articles/10.3389/fspor.2019.00010/full.

juggle everything becomes an asset when the scholar-athlete proceeds toward a career after they are finished playing their respective sport.

To be successful in career transition, athletes must proactively focus on the importance, awareness, and marketability of transferable skills (McKnight, 2007). The scholar-athlete tool kit includes: (a) Teamwork—a person learns to get along with, work with and connect with other people who are different from them in order to achieve a common greater purpose or goal; (b) Work ethic—a person develops a strong belief that there is value to working hard to achieve honorable goals, the process of which develops resiliency and strength of character; (c) Commitment—a person gains understanding that with every great freedom comes an even greater responsibility, and that commitment is required to bring your endeavors to a successful completion; (d) Leadership—a person gains the ability to inspire and constantly teach through their actions and their words; (e) Time management—a person must prioritize tasks effectively in order to meet deadlines and achieve worthy goals; and (f) Physical and emotional health—a person learns to recognize the importance of a whole and well-balanced lifestyle. The listed skill-set was compiled based on previous research of athletes who identified the most desirable skills and confirmed their existence (Petitpas et al., 1992; Danish et al., 1993; Mayocchi and Hanrahan, 2000; McKnight, 2007; Chalfin et al., 2015). Studies have supported the notion that athletes who capitalize on transferable skills are more likely to experience successful change between athletic and non-athletic settings (Blinde and Greendorfer, 1985). Collegiate coaches and administrators are always searching for an athletic edge, while faculty and admission offices are actively searching for the same type of academic excellence—prowess in the field is not only for sports, it is also for academics which takes many hours of mental agility, study, and hard work, skills not thought of in reference to scholar-athletes. The current academic-athletic rift is now in the process of widening on U.S. college campuses and in society as a whole. This contentious mindset starts with a limited and distorted view regarding what young people see as the pathway to success.

[...]

In U.S. higher education, there is a greater emphasis being placed on the athletic abilities of student-athletes and the success of their teams, rather than their success in the classroom (Harrison et al., 2010). College sports have increasingly become a popular form of mass commercial entertainment (Gerdy, 2006). Many elite high school athletes are seen on ESPN signing their national letter of intent, which is an NCAA document committing them to play at a specific institution. The primary purpose of higher education, which is to prepare individuals to make lifelong productive contributions to society, is overlooked far too often. As the popularity and social status of sport continues to rise, middle school and high school institutions are now facing the challenge of addressing an increasing lack of academic productivity among some student groups (Bowen and Levin, 2003). When athletic performance is more important than academic success, cultural perceptions then become more important than educational programs. The high ground needs to be retaken in order to challenge and transform the atudent-athlete's courage and vision for their own future.

For many young people in our neighborhood communities and schools, the path to success is seen solely through athletics (Taylor, 2018). This mindset now shapes how young people view the future. Structural and cultural factors, such as upward economic mobility, gender identity, media and street social interactions have an overwhelming influence on a young person's aspirations and expectations to pursue a professional career in sports (Baker et al., 2006). The present study calls for a basic recasting of these perceptions, including instilling in young people the viewpoints that: (a) all athletes are scholars; (b) most athletes should pursue academics over athletics as their primary future pathway toward achieving professional and economic success; (c) all athletes should consider their athletic ability as only one component of multiple dynamic dimensions of their identity; and (d) all athletes must consider themselves active scholarly participants in learning rather than passive uninvolved bystanders in the educational process. Our media and communities are saturated with individuals who have used their trained athletic skill-set to break down barriers of the status quo of race, class, gender as it relates to the scholar-athlete to become successful in professions other than sports. A few familiar examples include President Gerald Ford, Earvin "Magic" Johnson, and Shannon Miller. President Ford was born July 14, 1913, in Omaha, Nebraska, where his mother divorced his father just days after he was born and lived a few years as a single parent. Ford developed a love for football and attended the University of Michigan (1930–1934) where he played center, linebacker, and long snapper for the football team and helped lead the Wolverines to two undefeated seasons and back to back national titles in 1932 and 1933. After college he had an extremely successful career in politics and eventually served as the 38th President of the United States from 1974 to 1977 (Greene, 2019).

Earvin "Magic" Johnson was born August 14, 1959, in Lansing, Michigan, and lived in low-income housing with his nine siblings and raised by his father, Earvin Sr., a General Motors assembly worker and garbage collector, and mother Christine Johnson. Earvin developed a love for basketball at a young age and attended Michigan State University in East Lansing, where he led the Spartans to a national title during the 1978–79 season. Magic was drafted first overall in 1979 and played professional basketball as a point guard for the Los Angeles Lakers from 1979 to 1991, where he won five NBA championships. Since Johnson's (NBA Encyclopedia, 2019) retirement from basketball he has become an advocate for HIV/AIDS prevention, an entrepreneur running a conglomerate called

Magic Johnson Enterprises with a net worth of $700 million, and is part owner of the Los Angeles Lakers, Los Angeles Dodgers, and Los Angeles Sparks.

Shannon Miller was born March 10, 1977, in Rolla, Missouri. Even though gymnastics as a sport was not popular amongst youth, especially girls, Shannon's parents decided to get her involved at the early age of five and soon had her traveling all over the world. Shannon became a USA Olympic icon in gymnastics. In the 1992 Olympic Games in Barcelona, Miller came away with five Olympic medals. Then again in 1996 she was a co-captain of the "Magnificent Seven" for Team USA who won the first Olympic Team Gold for Women's Gymnastics in United States history. After retiring at the age of 19 from Olympic competition, Miller (Wikipedia, 2019a) received her undergraduate degrees in marketing and entrepreneurship from the University of Houston and her law degree from Boston College. In 2010 Miller launched a company called Shannon Miller Lifestyle: Health and Fitness for Women, which advocates for the health and wellness of women and children. In addition to these types of examples of elite athletes, there are significant stories of innumerable other athletes who used their trained athletic skill-set to break down the barriers of the usual state of opinion in reference to race, class, gender as it relates to the scholar-athlete. These individuals have also competed at different intercollegiate levels in which many times is neither seen on television or read about in social media outlets, yet they have effectively applied their athletic skill-set to succeed in professional endeavors outside of their sport.

The scholar-athlete is an individual that participates in and fully explores his or her ability to achieve excellence in both academics and a sport. The incredible availability and ever-changing array of technological resources that young people have at their fingertips offer great opportunities for them to do research, explore, and even problem solve. The scholarly interactions experienced by all young athletes prepare them for the entirety of their future lives. Furthermore, scholarly activities motivate and inspire young people (Yazzie-Mintz, 2007). Detachment from scholarly pursuits leads to a lack of motivation, falling behind in work, truancy, teenage pregnancy, caring for a family member and student boredom (Hudson, 2017). This psychological disengagement becomes manifested as resistance to schooling and higher dropout rates (Caldwell et al., 1999). Unfortunately, these feelings of disengagement are commonly passed on from adults to children, resulting in the development of deep-seated resistance to education (Adelman and Taylor, 2011). A further result is the feeling of boredom for all aspects of their personal and professional lives. Misplaced priorities have created barriers to student-athlete learning and personal development, and calls for reform (Bedford, 2007). To that end, once a person has become an engaged scholar, the individual gains the curiosity and motivation required for a fulfilling future life. When instructors adequately engage with students, they begin to recognize the potential benefits of learning through the use of practical issues that relate to the scholar's real experiences and personal spaces of knowledge that have roots in the reality in which they live. Scholars stay interested, learn more, and develop a desire to participate in the subject when techniques are used to involve them in collaborative learning projects (Yazzie-Mintz, 2007). Worldwide there is a growing commitment to best practices that engage students starting in middle school in discussions of scholarly teaching and research (Oseguera, 2010).

[...]

College Sports Is a Corrupt Mega-Business

George Leef

George Leef is director of editorial content for the James G. Martin Center for Academic Renewal. He has published numerous articles in The Freeman, Reason, The Free Market, Cato Journal, The Detroit News, Independent Review, *and* Regulation.

College sports are a gigantic entertainment business that have nothing to do with the missions of the schools. Frequently, the highest-paid employee of a school is the football or basketball coach, and the athletics budget is hugely subsidized by fees paid by financially strapped students. Players who read and write at a middle-school level (if even that) are recruited to help teams win, but the academic work they do is laughable. Schools rack up big debts trying to win glory on the gridiron or court, even if it means scrimping on faculty salaries and building maintenance.

How did this lamentable state of affairs come about?

To find out, the book to read is *Intercollegiate Athletics, Inc.* by professor James T. Bennett. He has researched the history of college sports in America, starting with the earliest days (when contests were organized and run by students for their own enjoyment) up to the latest scandals and perversions. He explains how the sports juggernaut gathered force (first football, later basketball) and recounts the various efforts (mostly unsuccessful) to stop or at least slow it. And perhaps most usefully, he points out that the high cost of college sports falls mainly on students through mandatory fees—a tax on education that goes to benefit a pampered few.

If you're bothered by the fact that, as the author reports on a recent study, Division I schools (the top level in the NCAA's hierarchy) spend three to six times as much on athletics per

"How College Sports Turned into a Corrupt Mega-Business," by George Leef, The James G. Martin Center for Academic Renewal, March 11, 2020. Reprinted by permission.

athlete as they do on academics per student, then this is a book you'll want to read.

The first intercollegiate sporting competition was not football, but rowing, when the Harvard and Yale teams met in 1852. Football started to gain popularity in the 1870s when students began organizing games between rival colleges. By the turn of the century, football was big. Winning had become so important that teams routinely brought in "ringers," which is to say, good players who weren't students at all. Injuries were common.

The first college presidents to speak out against this spectacle were Charles Eliot of Harvard and Nicholas Murray Butler of Columbia. Eliot criticized the "immoderate desire to win" that led to cheating and the militaristic aura surrounding football. At Columbia, Butler decided to abolish football in 1905, calling it an "academic nuisance" that interfered with studying. Butler's abolition lasted only a decade, however.

From the Northeast, football soon spread to the South and the Midwest, where the problems identified by Eliot and Butler grew apace. One academic leader who tried to tame football's malign influence was UNC president Frank Porter Graham. In 1935, he drew up a proposal to ban the recruitment of players and any preferential treatment of athletes in the awarding of scholarships, jobs, or loans.

How well was Graham's proposal received? Bennett quotes him as saying that his critics "opened up with machine guns, and in some cases poison gas." Attacked by alumni and many of the politicians who voted for UNC appropriations, Graham backed down quietly. Although he served until 1949, he never again attempted to do anything about the growing tumor of college football.

In the Midwest, the University of Chicago was king of the football realm in the 1920s and 1930s. The university's president, William Rainey Harper, hired the famous coach Amos Alonzo Stagg and gave him carte blanche to win. Stagg did exactly that. His methods were often unscrupulous, but the "Monsters of the Midway" became a powerhouse. But when Robert Maynard Hutchins was named president in1929, he was extremely unhappy with the situation. He thought that sports should be merely an ancillary function of a university. "A college racing stable makes as much sense as college football," he said.

Under Hutchins, Chicago instituted a rule that football players had to take the same courses as all other students, and that pulled the rug out from under Stagg's mighty team. By 1939, it was a doormat, losing by such scores as 61-0 to Harvard and 85-0 to Michigan. At the end of that season, Hutchins announced that Chicago would drop intercollegiate football.

In a speech to the students, he explained his reasons: "I hope that it is not necessary for me to tell you that this is an educational institution, that education is primarily concerned with the training of the mind, and that athletics and social life, though they may contribute to it, are not the heart of it and cannot be permitted to interfere with it."

To the saga of Chicago football, Bennett adds this humorous ending: "The Maroons locker room would be converted to house the Manhattan Project, giving a new meaning to the phrase long bomb."

We learn that several other universities have also dropped football, including the University of Seattle and the University of Denver. Getting out of that costly extravaganza is feasible, although a university president who proposes it must be ready for fierce opposition.

Consider the tale of Ray Watts, president of the University of Alabama at Birmingham (UAB). Football is almost a state religion in Alabama, but UAB wasn't very successful and program costs were heavily subsidized by student fees and the university's general budget. In 2014, looking at a bleak financial picture, Watts decided that the money football was absorbing would be better spent on academics and announced that the university was dropping the sport.

Poor President Watts—he hadn't counted on the ferocious opposition to his pro-academic priorities. He was roasted in the press, excoriated by the alumni, and even the faculty lashed out with a vote of no confidence. To save his hide, Watts reversed field. After a fundraising drive brought in $20 million, he announced that football would be back in 2017. It is back, and so are the high costs.

On the other hand, if a college president wants to add big-time sports or move up to a "higher" conference, he'll find plenty of support. He can hire consulting firms to produce "research" that will demonstrate how a sports move will have great long-term benefits. In such studies, the costs are always downplayed while the supposed benefits (such as increased school loyalty) are hyped.

This has "worked" at a number of schools, including UNC-Charlotte. In 2007, chancellor Philip Dubois decided that his school's reputation would soar if it started playing top-level football. He got his way. Millions were spent to build the necessary stadium and hire the coaches. Student fees went from an already lofty $1,160 per student to $1,648. Since starting play in the Sunbelt Conference in 2008, UNCC teams haven't won many games, but even if they had, is there any reason to believe that the institution would be the least bit better? Bennett doesn't think so.

But sometimes common sense prevails and the idea of boosting school prestige through sports is shot down. One such case was at another UNC institution, Winston-Salem State. The administration foolishly committed to moving up to NCAA Division I in 2007. But three years into its transition, a new chancellor concluded that the cost, which included $10 million in facility upgrades, was not justified and the school went back to competing in Division II. No sense in throwing good money after bad.

Bennett's penultimate chapter explores the way women's sports have followed the ruinous path of men's athletics, beginning in the 1970s. That topic merits a separate article.

And that brings us to the ultimate chapter: "Reform—or Renewal?"

Bennett is not optimistic that college sports will change for the better. Few college presidents have the backbone for a fight with the entrenched athletics establishment, the faculty is generally not interested in battling it, and hardly any students care much about the cost that athletics adds to their bills. How about federal intervention? Bennett mentions some legislative ideas that have been floating around Congress but isn't enthusiastic about any.

How about paying college athletes? Bennett gives that idea the back of his hand. He writes, "If college football and basketball players do join the ranks of the officially salaried, we will have the strange spectacle of ordinary students paying increased fees in order to subsidize not just the education but the livelihoods, the salaries, of their far more feted and celebrated sports-playing fellow 'students.' And if you pay those who play revenue sports, the big-time sports factories may need to shutter non-revenue sports, which would run afoul of Title IX."

If you read *Intercollegiate Athletics, Inc.* you'll be convinced that we have a serious problem, but also that it's a problem with no evident solution.

Sports and College Are Incompatible

Josh Edwards

Josh Edwards covers college football and the NFL for 247Sports. He has a baccalaureate degree from Ohio University and a master's degree from Xavier University.

College sports programs were developed as a supplement to the academic experience, a means by which to foster in young students an appreciation for teamwork, competition, public spiritedness, and a sense of fair play. As time has passed, though, big-time college sports have become a revenue generating form of mass entertainment, making sports programs a primary vehicle through which many universities chase status and money. It could hardly be otherwise. Division 1-A football teams average revenue of around $30 million annually, while the very best teams cash in at close to $200 million.[1] In 2018, the U.S. Department of Education (USDOE) estimated that post-secondary college sports raked in $14.2 billion in revenue, up from $4 billion in 2003, and more than every professional sports league except the National Football League.[2]

While most colleges contend that their sports programs fail to make a profit, it has become clear that the survival of many sports programs require, at the very least, a softening of traditional academic standards.[3] This too could hardly be otherwise. Mass entertainment amateur sports require top-level athletes, not scholars, and the incentive to excel academically is not typically enough to attract the very best. Thus, the weakening of academic standards imposed by the athletics regime is an inherent feature of the mismatch between the goals of educational institutions and that of high revenue, mass entertainment sports.

Recent serious and regrettable scandals, along with a number of high profile legal challenges to the college sports system, have thrust this mismatch into the glaring light of day, and may provide an opening through which necessary reforms could advance.

Corrupt Curricula

The University of North Carolina (UNC) scandal of 2010 illustrates how big-time sports programs can corrupt the academic mission. The scandal involved not only lowering academic requirements for student athletes, but the actual creation of a subpar program of study designed to preserve the athletic eligibility of student athletes.

The practice of carving out inferior academic niches in the form of new, less rigorous courses—or even whole departments and degree programs—for underprepared students is not new. A recent study by the National Association of Scholars documents that the rise of African American Studies degree programs were a response, in part, to the presence in large numbers of underprepared black students resulting from preferential admissions. The study notes, "[t]he admission of substantial numbers of black students was inextricably linked with the pressure to create the Afro-American Studies program."[4] Similar kinds of efforts to provide substandard academic coursework for underprepared student athletes has also become common, with UNC's effort being only the most publicized.

At UNC roughly 200 courses were created within the African and Afro-American studies department to support student athletes ill-equipped to maintain good academic standing along traditional lines. As a university-commissioned investigation explained, UNC had for nearly two decades offered a "shadow curriculum" of fake classes into which athletes were steered. A single staff member administered most of these courses—skirting common checks and balances in the grading system—course requirements were minimal and grades, the investigation found, were often changed without authorization. Most of the participating students were from the high profile, big money sports of basketball and football and, as the *New York Times* reported in 2017, the scheme "appeared to be a stark subversion of the NCAA's central tenet that college athletics are a mere component of education."[5]

The NCAA filed several "notices of allegations" against UNC beginning in 2014 and by 2018 the university had spent $21 million on legal fees.[6] UNC maintained that the fraudulent courses were open to all students, only marginally involved university athletics, and that the problems were academic in nature, and therefore beyond the NCAA's purview.[7] In the end the NCAA agreed, taking no action and stating that it lacked the power to punish the university under the rules of the NCAA. Similar misconduct, UNC officials noted, was also alleged at Auburn University and the University of Michigan, two other major sports schools, and the NCAA chose not to penalize those schools either.

In the aftermath of the scandal, UNC officials insisted that it had "done everything possible to correct and move beyond the past academic irregularities." But critics of UNC and the NCAA were dismayed. UNC history professor Jay M. Smith was so disappointed in the outcome of the investigation that he co-authored a book about the scandal entitled *Cheated* (2015), and created a new course to teach UNC students about it—History 383: Big-Time College Sports and the Rights of Athletes 1874 to Present.[8] "I thought, I cannot rely on this institution to do the right thing," Smith told the *New York Times*, "and I think it would be an abdication of responsibility for us to pass up the opportunity to provide students at this institution an opportunity to learn about their scandal."[9]

The consequences for students of putting athletics before academics at UNC appear to have been traumatic. Learning specialist Mary Willingham, co-author with Smith of *Cheated*, surveyed 183 UNC athletes who participated in either football or men's basketball from 2004-2012. She found that 60 percent read at between a fourth and eighth grade level. Between eight and ten percent read below a third grade level.[10] "The focus is on keeping an athlete eligible rather than letting them have access to a real desired education," said B. David Ridpath, a professor of sports administration at Ohio University who now works at The Drake Group, which advocates for academic accountability in college sports.[11] Another writer explained succinctly about Division I athletes in general, "They are steered into meaningless classes with 'safe' professors; they plagiarize; they get illicit tutoring—whatever it takes to retain eligibility. Many coaches, alumni, administrators and faculty facilitate the charade."[12]

The Power of Sports on Campus

While the UNC scandal involved the degradation of coursework in order to keep underprepared athletes enrolled, the recent scandal dubbed "Operation Varsity Blues" (OVB) exposed the problem of admitting athletes without the requisite academic credentials. As with the creation of a two-tiered system of course work, lowering admissions standards in order to admit underprepared students (or to exclude disfavored ones) has a long pedigree in U.S. colleges, dating back at least to the Ivy League's "Jewish Quotas" of the 1920s. The system of admissions preferences for black and Hispanic applicants and for children of alumni ("legacies") is to this day perhaps the most divisive issue in higher education. Preferences for student athletes is, in other words, part of a much broader and more fundamental debate over the university's role as the gatekeeper of opportunity and success.

Nevertheless, OVB has revealed to the world how thoroughly sports programs and the people who run them have consolidated their power over university admissions policy, at the expense not only of academic quality but of equal opportunity as well.

In March 2019, federal prosecutors in the Office of the U.S. Attorney for the District of Massachusetts unsealed indictments of fifty people on conspiracy and fraud charges relating to a college admissions scheme spanning several top tier and second tier institutions across the country. The case riveted the public's attention not only because it involved well-known celebrities Lori Laughlin (of television's *Full House*) and Felicity Huffman (*Desperate Housewives*), but also because it reinforced a fashionable but powerful media-driven narrative of class warfare, in which the rich and famous play by a different set of rules.

At the center of the scandal, parents paid William Singer, a college admissions consultant—through his charitable venture Key Worldwide Foundation—to inflate their child's ACT or SAT scores in order to make acceptance to colleges of their choice more likely.[13]

Of the fifty people charged in connection with the scandal, thirteen were college coaches charged with accepting bribes in return for their help conjuring false athletic profiles of Singer's clients. Singer himself dubbed the bribing of athletic coaches a "side door" through which he could gain access for his clients to colleges. Unlike the case of UNC, in which the institution's curriculum standards were challenged, OVB demonstrated how the compromise of admissions standards—perhaps the primary screening mechanism for which employers rely on universities—for athletes can be exploited by those with the resources to do so. The scandal will likely serve to raise the level of skepticism with which potential employers view the value of degrees granted by these institutions, a skepticism already heightened by such practices as grade inflation and the creation of academically vacuous degree programs.

Most revealing about the OVB scandal was not that Singer could so easily game the system, or that so many athletic coaches were corruptible, but that coaches of even low-revenue, small-market sports programs could wield such influence over closely guarded admissions policies. The FBI report revealed, for example, that one of those indicted was a water polo coach at the University of Southern California, who insisted in an email to his athletic director that a Singer client "would be the fastest player on our team." Of course, the client's athletic prowess was fabricated by Singer, who was paid tens of thousands of dollars to do so. Along with water polo, indicted college officials cultivated by Singer included coaches of sports like sailing, soccer, and tennis.

The power of big-time college sports coaches on university campuses is common knowledge, and hardly mysterious. No one was surprised, for example, when Joe Paterno took the brunt of the blame at Penn State in 2011, when an FBI sting nabbed a retired assistant football coach who was sexually molesting children for fifteen years. For forty-five years (1966-2011) Paterno coached a Nittany Lions football program that brought in—even after the scandal—roughly $140 million in annual revenue.[14] Unsurprisingly, former FBI director Louis Freeh issued a university-sponsored report on the scandal that found "[a]t the heart of the problem were university leaders eager to please Paterno above all else."[15]

But most schools do not share in this kind of sports generated wealth, and water polo teams don't bring them any closer to doing so. In truth, though, neither do high level football or basketball programs. Roughly 75 percent of the NCAA's estimated $1.3 billion in net profit (after expenses estimated by the USDOE of about $12.9 billion), goes to the Power Five conferences (ACC, Big Ten, Big XII, PAC-12 and SEC),[16] representing just sixty-five out of 350 schools in Division I and more than 1,000 schools in the NCAA all together. It is estimated now that only about twenty college athletics programs nationwide consistently make a profit, and finances are probably worst for public institutions. A review of the data by the International Business Times found that "[m]ost public universities lose money on their athletic programs."[17]

Sports and Campus Pride

While the sixty-five Power Five conference institutions want to win and acquire the greatest amount of revenue possible in the process, the motive for most schools in funding both big and small athletic programs goes beyond direct financial benefit.[18] Schools obviously feel pressure by broadcasters, gamblers, corporate sponsors, food purveyors, athlete representatives, transport companies, facilities architects, and other stakeholders who suckle at the multibillion dollar teat of college sports. But for most campuses the benefits of sports programs is less directly about revenue generation and more about the way in which sports help build community support for the institution.[19]

Just observe what happens when a school attempts to eliminate a money-losing sports program. In 2014, when the University of Alabama-Birmingham announced that its football program was being cut because of financial difficulties, school president Ray Watts had to be escorted by police from the meeting at which the announcement was made. Players cried and Watts received large amounts of hate mail. Most importantly, alumni responded by donating large amounts of money in support of the football program. In two years' time, $42 million flowed into the school to support the football program, enough to cover operations for five years. Jim Livengood, a veteran Division I athletics director, explained "[f]ootball is part of the culture in that state and that city. It was in the fiber of Birmingham, and you saw that in the initial response."[20]

For generations, sports teams have functioned as conduits through which colleges can nurture powerful emotional attachments and feelings of kinship, the necessary precursors for establishing brand loyalty, notoriety, donations and, eventually, future generations of applicants. What is new is the desperately heightened importance this role has taken on as higher education has drifted from its traditional purpose. Degree programs have proliferated and the reasons for students being at a campus have grown wildly divergent. Students are now drawn from a dizzying array of backgrounds for a seemingly infinite number of educational purposes. Only about half of all students are even drawn from the traditional 17 to 21 year-old age category.[21] Seventy-three percent are now considered "non-traditional," meaning they either work while attending school, study part-time or online, or support a family.[22]

The unifying and socializing role of college sports has grown commensurate with increasingly disaggregated campuses. But the fragmentation of college life resulting from this sweeping repurposing has been nowhere near as divisive as higher education's movement—full bore—into cultural politics. As colleges and universities became demographically diverse—Hispanics alone rose from 4 percent to 17 percent of all U.S. residents enrolled in degree-granting programs between 1976 and 2015. Asians make up over 20 percent of enrolled undergraduates at most elite colleges. Females now receive close to 60 percent of all baccalaureate degrees[23]—universities worked overtime to ensure separate identities for these newer demographic groups. Before long, campuses were replete with gender and ethnic studies programs, racially segregated dorms, and separate commencement ceremonies. The National Association of Scholars 2019 study *Separate but Equal, Again* found that about 46 percent of 173 colleges surveyed segregate student orientation programs; 43 percent offer segregated residential arrangements; and 72 percent segregate graduation ceremonies.[24] At the same time, Title IX sexual harassment policies, the creation of "safe spaces," the adoption of restrictive speech codes, and the establishment of diversity bureaucracies have turned college campuses into simmering culture war zones. As author Jason Richwine has noted, "University campuses have become microcosms of interethnic disputes in American society . . . The difference, however, is that the wealthy and protective campus environment enables such disputes to be more strident."[25]

The traditional responsibility of colleges and universities for fostering useful knowledge and critical thinking skills in young adults has receded as the goals of achieving mass access, monopolizing control over accreditation, and adjudicating racial, gender, and sexual grievances have advanced. The result is the disappearance of a shared college experience. Sports programs—even revenue-losing sports programs—have gained their power over university life, in other words, almost in direct proportion to the exploding multifunctional and politicized nature of college life itself.[26] It is for this reason that Charles Clotfelter, in his 2011 study *Big-Time Sports in American Universities* (2011), identified "school spirit" as one of the five top reasons colleges fund sports programs: "Few aspects of college life create a sense of community on a campus like prominent athletics teams."[27]

Amateurism

Nothing is more central to the fulfillment of its unifying role than the commitment of college sports to amateurism.[28] The amateur student-athlete, enrolled in school and competing on behalf of the college is what piques the public interest and generates the revenue that has enriched stakeholders. The NCAA has itself claimed that college sports would devolve into a second-rate imitator of minor league sports without amateurism, writing in a recent court brief, "despite the abundance of professional minor leagues such as Minor League Baseball and the NBA G League filled with very skilled athletes, none has ever attracted anything close to the popularity of college sports."[29]

But amateurism in college athletics has been a farce for years, and it is the central myth by which colleges and universities have been able to marry the educational mission to the completely unrelated enterprise of mass entertainment sports, to the great detriment of higher education. While the best college athletes are not paid directly (as amateurism requires), they are feted as campus celebrities, excused from rigorous course work, train in world class facilities under the best coaches, and are relieved of most student related expenses so that they can devote as much time to their craft as most professional athletes. The falsehood that world class athletes can play for colleges while living the life of diligent undergraduates, all in return for the privilege of receiving a baccalaureate degree, has allowed universities to undermine the academic mission of colleges.

Is Change Possible?

There is every indication that a system that does not pay college athletes a reasonable portion of the revenue they generate is unsustainable. Several prominent critics have suggested reforming the system to pay college athletes on Division I teams directly. In 2011, civil rights historian Taylor Branch suggested just such a direct payment scheme, predictably lambasting the current system as carrying the "unmistakable whiff of the plantation," but offering little in the way of details.[30] Joe Nocera, writing in the *New York Times Magazine*, offered a five point plan that also pays Division I college basketball and football players, but tipped his partisan hat by transfixing on establishing "lifetime health insurance" for athletes under the auspice of a powerful player's union.[31] In March of 2019, U.S. Representative Mark Walker of North Carolina introduced federal legislation—"The Student-Athlete Equity Act"—that would remove restrictions from a student-athlete being compensated for use of their name, image and likeness.[32]

Nevertheless, the courts seem reluctant to carry out this kind of reform. In a 2014 ruling in a case brought by a Division I basketball player over payments made to the NCAA for selling players' likenesses to a video game company, judge Claudia Wilken ruled that the NCAA's rules on amateurism violated antitrust laws. Wilken held that schools should be allowed to pay athletes the full cost of attendance (covering cost of living expenses) not previously accounted for in player scholarships. While a 2015 U.S. Circuit Court of Appeals overturned Wilken's finding that players could receive up to $5,000 a year in stipends,[33] it agreed that college athletes could be paid for the use of their names, images and likenesses, but in very limited amounts. Also upheld was an option to set up trusts to pay football and basketball players after their college careers were over.[34]

Five years after her decision, Wilken found herself presiding over a similar court case challenging the caps the NCAA put on student-athlete compensation. Wilken again agreed with the players that capping scholarship money is a violation of antitrust laws, ruling that the NCAA could not limit compensation "related to education."[35] This decision gave hope to the plaintiffs, and likely means higher payments for things like tuition, books, room and board, fees, graduate school, and the "cost of attendance." But it fell short of allowing the market-rate, direct compensation that the plaintiffs wanted.[36]

Most importantly, perhaps, the court refused to relinquish the ideal of the amateur student-athlete. "The court does credit the importance to consumer demand of maintaining a distinction between college sports and professional sports," Wilken wrote. The case has been stayed pending an NCAA appeal.[37]

But even if the federal courts do eventually allow direct payment of student-athletes, the underlying corruption inherent in coupling higher education to big-time college sports will remain. Because of the high level of fan and alumni support that Division I college sports enjoy, and because athletes would still be enrolled as students, colleges will be incentivized to shape funding and academic programming around Division I football and basketball. Colleges and universities would still need to offer scholarships and subpar academic programs to athletes who are ill-equipped academically. As long as colleges and universities offer degrees to athletes who don't earn them, corruption is inevitable.[38]

For that reason there should be a complete legal and institutional break between the universities and Division I sports teams. This will leave Division II and Division III college sports programs to fulfill the Knute Rockne ideal of students playing for school pride. The plan put forward by Richard DeMillo of the James G. Martin Center for Academic Renewal seems the most promising. DeMillo argues that Division I college sports should be separated by a legislative "corporate firewall" from academics, a "Glass-Steagall" Act for Division I football and basketball, a reference to the Depression-era legislation that separated commercial banking from investment banking. All Division I college sports teams under DeMillo's plan would become separate corporations licensed by the university, but having no further relationship with it. Licensed corporations would hire athletes and pay for training and other operating and capital expenses. None of the associated costs would be carried on university accounts. Just as a university uses a subcontractor to redesign its dormitories or create a university clothing line, so would Division I sports corporations be a subcontractor of the university. The incentives of coaches, university presidents, sports teams, advertisers, television networks and the rest to exploit the talents of the athletes for their value, while depriving them of their fair share and forcing them into the role of student, would disappear. Those Division I athletes that have no interest in going to college won't have to. Those that do would be transformed into work-study students. "They would join the ranks of countless engineering, journalism, and business students who spend part of the year working at a company, developing skills, building the professional networks, and earning money for tuition, fees, and books," writes DeMillo.[39]

Yes, under a plan like DeMillo's, the Zion Williamsons and Trevor Lawrences would no longer grace the purely amateur college athletic games carried on by Division II and Division III clubs, but as long as competition is close and fandom exists, little will change. And Division I sports corporations will, in all likelihood, retain Division I college popularity. Remember the backlash against the Olympics when they began allowing professional athletes to take part in competition during the 1980s. Those concerns quickly dissipated as professional athletes were adopted as part of the practice. The same future could be in store for the NCAA.

It is possible to alter the current structure of college sports. "I've seen things change that are far more complicated and far more of a struggle to flip around," David Ridpath has said. There are multiple models that could be implemented but it is hard to envision the current structure remaining intact. Ridpath again: "The first thing that we have to do is accept that what we are doing now is not working. It sure as heck is not going to work much longer."[40]

Notes

1. Cork Gaines, "The average college football team makes more money than the next 25 college sports combined," *Business Insider*, October 20, 2016.
2. U.S. Department of Education, Equity in Athletics Data Analysis, retrieved on May 18, 2019 from https://ope.ed.gov/athletics/Trend/public/#/answer/6/601/main?row=-1&column=1; Chris Murphy, *Madness Inc. How Everyone Is Getting Rich off College Sports Except the Players*, Chris Murphy, U.S. Senator for Connecticut, retrieved on May 18, 2019 from https://www.murphy.senate.gov/download/madness-inc; Darren Ravell, "NCAA tops $1 billion in revenue during 2016-17 school year," ESPN.com, March 7, 2018, http://www.espn.com/college-sports/story/_/id/22678988/ncaa-tops-1-billion-revenue-first
3. Matt Brown, "Major college athletic departments have money. Be skeptical when they say otherwise," SBnation.com, February 28, 2019, https://www.sbnation.com/2019/2/28/18242974/college-sports-athletic-department-profit-revenue-money
4. Dion J. Pierre, Peter W. Wood, *Neo-Segregation at Yale*, in *Separate but Equal, Again: Neo-Segregation in American Higher Education* (New York: National Association of Scholars: 2019), 39, https://www.nas.org/images/documents/NeoSegregation_at_Yale.pdf
5. The NCAA is the National Collegiate Athletics Association. Marc Tracy, "N.C.A.A.: North Carolina Will Not Be Punished for Academic Scandal," *New York Times*, October 13, 2017.
6. Dan Kane, "New Legal Bills Push UNC's Tab for Academic Scandal to $21 Million," *News & Observer*, August 14, 2018.
7. Tracy.
8. Marc Tracy, "College Sports 101: A U.N.C. Class Reviews a Scandal at Its Source," *New York Times*, April 4, 2019.
9. Ibid.

10. Sara Ganim, "Some College Athletes Play Like Adults, Read Like 5th-graders," CNN, January 8, 2014.

11. B. David Ridpath, "The College Football Playoff and Other NCAA Revenues Are an Exposé of Selfish Interest," *Forbes*, January 17, 2017.

12. Jay Schalin, "Time for universities to punt football," *Washington Times*, September 1, 2011.

13. Amy B. Wang, Des Bieler, "College Coaches Took Bribes to Pass Kids Off as Star Athletes, FBI Says. The NCAA Is Investigating," *Washington Post*, March 13, 2019.

14. Ben Jones, "Penn State Football Generated More Than $100 Million in Revenue in 2017-18," Statecollege.com, February 6, 2019; "Penn State Scandal Fast Facts," CNN.com, February 9, 2019.

15. Ann O'Neill, "The woman who stood up to Joe Paterno," CNN.com, July 30, 2012.

16. Acronyms in order, Atlantic Coast Conference, the Big Ten Conference (headquartered in Chicago), The Big 12 (headquartered in Texas), Pacific Coast Conference, Southeastern Conference.

17. Gerald Gurney, Donna A. Lopiano, Andrew Zimbalist, *Unwinding Madness: What Went Wrong with College Sports and How to Fix It* (Washington, D.C.: Brookings Institution Press, 2017), 28; David Sirota, "College Football: Public Universities Spend Millions on Stadiums, Despite Slim Chance For Payoff," *International Business Times*, January 1, 2016; John Thelin, "Paying College Athletes," *InsideHigherEd*, February 12, 2019; Mary Gormandy White, "Does College Football Make Money?," LovetoKnow.com, May 10, 2019, https://college.lovetoknow.com/campus-life/does-college-football-make-money

18. Robert H. Frank, "Challenging the Myth: A Review of the Links Among College Athletic Success, Student Quality, and Donations," Knight Foundation Commission on Intercollegiate Athletics (May 2004).

19. James P. Melcher, "How do most colleges justify losing money on sports programs?" Quora.com, November 5, 2018, https://www.quora.com/How-do-most-colleges-justify-losing-money-on-sports-programs

20. Eben Novy-Williams, "Football is forever: The money-losing drug these schools can't quit," *Chicago Tribune*, January 6, 2017.

21. Peter McPherson, "Our college students are changing. Why aren't our higher education policies?," *Washington Post*, June 6, 2017, https://www.washingtonpost.com/opinions/our-college-students-are-changing-why-arent-our-higher-education-policies/2017/06/06/1fc0e37c-3678-11e7-b412-62beef8121f7_story.html?utm_term=.fe7ff1b37971

22. Destiny One, "Four Recent Changes That Have Radically Altered the Higher Education Landscape," Destiny Solutions," May 8, 2019, https://destinysolutions.com/four-recent-changes-that-have-radically-altered-the-higher-education-landscape/

23. "Fast Facts," National Center for Education Statistics, May 7, 2019, https://nces.ed.gov/fastfacts/display.asp?id=98; Jeff Guo, "Women are dominating men at college. Blame sexism," *Washington Post*, December 11, 2014.

24. Pierre, Wood.
25. Jason Richwine, "Low-Skilled Immigration and the Balkanized Campus," *Academic Questions* 31, no. 4, Winter 2018.
26. James P. Melcher, "How do most colleges justify losing money on sports programs?" Quora.com, November 5, 2018, https://www.quora.com/How-do-most-colleges-justify-losing-money-on-sports-programs
27. Charles T. Clotfelter, "Big-Time Sports in American Universities" (Cambridge University Press, 2011).
28. John V. Lombardi, "The Amateur Challenge of College Sports," *Inside Higher Ed.*, August 10, 2008, https://www.insidehighered.com/blogs/reality-check/amateur-challenge-college-sports
29. Michael McCann, "Stakes and Stakeholders in Alston v. NCAA, the Latest College Sports Antitrust Case," *Sports Illustrated*, September 4, 2018.
30. Taylor Branch, "The Shame of College Sports," *Atlantic* (October, 2011).
31. Joe Nocera, "Let's Start Paying College Athletes," *New York Times Magazine*, December 30, 2011.
32. "Walker Introduces Student-Athlete Equity Act to End NCAA Restrictions on Player's Publicity Rights," Congressman Mark Walker, March 19, 2019, https://walker.house.gov/media-center/press-releases/walker-introduces-student-athlete-equity-act-end-ncaa-restrictions
33. "Judge Rules Against NCAA in Federal Antitrust Lawsuit," *Wall Street Journal*, March 9, 2019.
34. Alex Kirshner, "Don't blame Ed O'Bannon for the death of the video games. Blame the NCAA," SBNation.com, July 13, 2018; Tom Farrey, "Players, Game Makers Settle for $40M," ESPN.com, May 31, 2014, http://www.espn.com/espn/otl/story/_/id/11010455/college-athletes-reach-40-million-settlement-ea-sports-ncaa-licensing-arm; "NCAA agrees to pay $208 million settlement in antitrust case," *Chicago Tribune*, February 4, 2017.
35. Michael McCann, "The NCAA's Latest Court Battle: How Much Can Schools Offer?" SI.com, September 4, 2018.
36. Dennis Dodd, "Judge rules NCAA can't cap athlete compensation 'related to education,' neither side happy with decision," CBS Sports, March 9, 2019.
37. Marc Tracy, "Judge Opens the Door to More Compensation for College Athletes," *New York Times*, March 9, 2019.
38. Schalin.
39. Richard DeMillo, "Reforming College Sports," James G. Martin Center for Academic Renewal, January 20, 2012, https://www.jamesgmartin.center/2012/01/reforming-college-sports/
40. Phone conversation between author and David Ridpath, February 21, 2019.

The COVID Pandemic Is Exposing the Flaws in College Sports

Craig Garthwaite and Matthew J. Notowidigdo

Craig Garthwaite is an associate professor of strategy, the Herman Smith Research Professor in Hospital and Health Services Management, and director of health care at the Kellogg School of Management at Northwestern University. Matthew Notowidigdo is a professor of economics at the University of Chicago.

This year's college football season is shaping up to be vastly different from any other in history. While games are being played, crowds are exceptionally limited or nonexistent. Furthermore, there are simply fewer games—and there is no guarantee of a complete season for any school. The combination of these factors is costing universities tens of millions of dollars and upending the underlying business model of college sports. Universities across the country have already responded by ending many low-revenue sports. This has led to widespread lamentations about the decreased opportunities for intercollegiate athletes who play sports that cannot support themselves financially.

However, if we are serious about caring for intercollegiate athletes, we should begin by reconsidering the corrupt bargain at the heart of modern college sports—one that has been magnified by the pandemic. In a new National Bureau of Economic Research paper that we co-authored with Jordan Keener and Nicole Ozminkowski, we empirically investigate the economic business model of college sports. We find that the prevailing model rests on taking the money generated by athletes who are more likely to be Black and come from low-income neighborhoods and transferring it to sports played by

"The COVID-19 Pandemic Is Revealing the Regressive Business Model of College Sports," by Craig Garthwaite and Matthew J. Notowidigdo, The Brookings Institution, October 16, 2020. Reprinted by permission.

athletes who are more likely to be white and from higher-income neighborhoods. The money is also transferred to coaches and used for the construction of lavish (and perhaps overly lavish) athletic facilities. With COVID-19 shutting off the money spigot, schools are being forced to publicly acknowledge that their athletic departments depend on regressively transferring money from athletes who grew up poor to those who grew up in richer households and to wealthy coaches.

This has led a variety of policy proposals ranging from paying players directly to allowing players to profit off their name and image, breaking a longtime requirement of amateurism in university athletics. Three states have passed legislation that would allow athletes to participate in a range of activities ranging from endorsements to autograph signings. In response to these widespread policy initiatives, the NCAA this week introduced a set of far more limited proposals that would allow college athletes to earn revenue from third parties. But it remains to be seen exactly how these policies would be implemented, and to what extent it would resolve issues of financial inequities for student-athletes. Furthermore, these efforts fall short of the athlete's bill of rights that was recently proposed by members of the U.S. Senate.

The Business Models of College Sports

We begin by documenting that college sports operates under two distinct business models. These are documented in Figure 1 [not shown], which shows the relationship between a school's athletic department revenue and the percentage of that revenue that comes from the university. In the upper-left corner is a set of Division 1 schools that largely resemble the idealistic images of amateur student-athletes competing for school pride. These schools earn relatively low revenues overall, and a large amount of their financial support comes from the university.

A second set of schools—those in the lower-right corner—have exceptionally high revenues and nearly all of those funds are generated by athletic endeavors, activities such as ticket sales, television contracts, and merchandise sales. These schools are all members of the "Power Five" athletic conferences, a set of schools that have traditionally fielded high-quality athletic programs. From 2006 to 2016, athletic departments at these schools saw their revenue nearly double, rising from $3.5 billion to $6.7 billion.

This difference in business models suggests that optimal policy in this area should distinguish between these two distinct sets of schools when considering how athletes are compensated for their time and efforts. To that end, our subsequent analysis concentrates on the economics of the schools in these Power Five conferences. The athletic departments in these schools resemble commercial enterprises that are generating meaningful economic rents. However, the revenues are largely generated by a small set of athletes. We document that football and men's basketball generate six times more revenue than all other sports combined. These sports, however, enjoy only 1.3 times more spending than other sports at the same school.

This difference between revenues and expenditures demonstrates how the funds generated by football and men's basketball players fund all of the remaining intercollegiate sports at each school. We estimate that the money generated by football and men's basketball causes: increased spending on money-losing sports; higher salaries for coaches and administrators; and increased spending on athletic facilities. Today, the average school in a Power Five conference supports 20 sports, but only two sports consistently pay for themselves, and the revenue generated by these two sports supports the seemingly ever-increasing salaries for coaches and athletic department employees.

Consider the teams playing the greatest college football rivalry game—the University of Michigan and Ohio State University. (Editor's note: This fact is debatable. Authors' note: No, it is not.) When these teams met in 2008, their coaching staffs earned $6 million and $5.7 million, respectively. Just 10 years later, these salaries grew to $15.5 million and $17.3 million—a roughly 300% increase. Even the strength and conditioning coaches for each team earned $600,000 and $735,000 a year, respectively. Conversely, the athletes on the field received no salaries for their efforts.

While we support opposite sides of this rivalry, we are united in agreement that this salary growth reflects a system that maximizes profits by limiting intercollegiate athletes' compensation to no more than the cost of attending school. The schools share these excess profits with coaches, administrators, and money-losing sports.

Supporters of the current system offer several arguments in favor of the status quo. Some say it is the deal the athletes signed, without acknowledging that collusion among schools through the NCAA limits the options of young athletes. Others claim that supporting other sports, particularly those played by female athletes, has broader societal benefits. Some argue that college athletics is uniquely attractive to fans because of the disingenuous belief that the competitors are just like the other students. Finally, some argue the athletes are already paid because they receive athletic scholarships, as if paying someone any positive amount is sufficient.

A New Model That Shares Revenue with Athletes

These arguments overlook the fundamental injustice created by transferring revenue generated from two sports played disproportionately by Black athletes from poorer neighborhoods to sports where athletes are disproportionately white and from wealthier neighborhoods and to high-income coaches. To approximate the money at stake, we consider as a benchmark a hypothetical situation where athletes could collectively bargain to the same degree as their professional counterparts.

If players in football and men's basketball received a similar share of revenue as NFL and NBA players—roughly

50% of sports-related revenue—then each scholarship football player would earn $360,000 per year and each scholarship basketball player would earn $500,000 per year. If wages by position reflected the relative earnings by position observed in professional sports, the starting quarterbacks would earn $2.4 million per year on average. Even the lowest-paid football players would receive $140,000 per year.

Such a system would create winners and losers. We would expect slower growth in coaches' salaries and facilities spending, for example. After all, intercollegiate athletes are currently "paid" in part with ludicrously lavish athletic facilities, containing features such as lazy rivers and laser tag. Additionally, it may be difficult to continue to abide by Title IX regulations, which require schools to provide equal opportunities for male and female athletes.

Title IX has had numerous positive effects and addressed many clear, historical, gender-based inequities in scholastic athletics. This is true at both the college and the secondary school level. However, optimal policy must consider that equity is a multifaceted concern that involves not just gender, but also important issues such as race and income. When viewed in this light, we believe our estimates demonstrate that, even after one considers the positive benefits for female athletes, the equity of Title IX when applied to an athletic department primarily supported by the efforts for poorer Black athletes is questionable at best. Any effort to reform the NCAA must consider a more nuanced regulatory approach that acknowledges the regressivity and racial injustice that is central to modern college sports.

However, allowing some intercollegiate athletes to share in the fruits of the labor does not stand in the way of continuing to provide meaningful athletic opportunities for athletes participating in sports that currently generate negative net incomes. To illustrate this point, consider that much of the growth in athletic department revenues since 2005 is driven by the increasingly valuable media rights for football and men's basketball. This includes both contracts with traditional networks like ESPN as well as the development of conference-owned channels, such as the Big Ten and SEC networks. This revenue growth is largely unrelated to the athletic success of other sports.

In Figure 2 [not shown], we show a comparison between the average actual spending on women's sports (the solid line) and estimated spending if the costs of these sports had only grown with inflation (the dashed line) for each school in a Power Five conference. This inflation-adjusted spending is an estimate of the resources necessary for a school to both provide athletic opportunities for female athletes, as well as increase revenue sharing for the athletes necessary to continue providing athletic opportunities for women's sports at the 2006 quality level. For the average school, the difference in this spending amounts to approximately $76,000 per scholarship athlete in football or men's basketball. This thought experiment demonstrates that there is ample revenue to both continue offering non-revenue sports at some level while compensating those responsible for the large growth in funds available to athletic departments.

The pandemic has pulled back the curtain on the ugly business of college sports. Its leaders would like to pretend it remains an amateur endeavor, but they only want to apply those cherished principles of amateurism to the athletes risking their health to generate profits, and not the coaches and administrators who financially benefit from the current system. Addressing this question is even more important as we ask college football players to risk their health to generate the money necessary to perpetuate this fundamentally inequitable system.

Current Controversies

Chapter 2

Are College Coaches, Administrators, and Other Officials Overpaid and Left Unchecked?

Overview: Are College Football Coaches Overpaid?

Arnold Loewy and Charles Moster

Arnold Loewy is the George Killiam Professor of Law at Texas Tech School of Law. Charles Moster is a former litigation attorney in the Ronald Reagan and George H. W. Bush presidential administrations.

This week, Arnold Loewy and Charles Moster debate whether college football coaches are overpaid. Moster is a former litigation attorney in the Ronald Reagan and George H. W. Bush presidential administrations who has offices in Lubbock, Amarillo, Midland/Odessa, Abilene and Georgetown, and Loewy is the George Killiam Professor of Law at Texas Tech School of Law.

Arnold: Winning coaches make schools big money

The topic of our debate today is whether major college football coaches are overpaid. Intuitively one might want to say "yes." After all, at practically all major football schools, the coach makes more than the president or chancellor of the university, and at state schools he makes more than the governor. In many places he makes more than five times the salary of the highest paid professor on campus.

Having said that, I do not believe football coaches, at least successful ones, are overpaid. The reason is simple economics 101. If what they do brings in more money than what they cost, they are a good value for the university. The difficulty is ascertaining how much money they make for the university.

Some of the money is measurable, i.e. revenue from sale of tickets and television. Unquestionably, as the phrase is used, good football teams put "butts in seats." Obviously, the more successful the team is, the more it can charge for the seats and the higher

"It's Debatable: Are College Football Coaches Overpaid?" *Lubbock Avalanche-Journal*, November 10, 2017. Reprinted by permission.

the percentage of seats that will be filled. At many schools, the revenue from football and basketball is sufficient to support the entire athletic department.

But this isn't half of what a successful football program means to a great university. A good football program can send alumni contributions through the roof. I recall when I was at a law professors' conference way back in the 1970s, a friend of mine from the University of Pittsburgh told me about his law school's new building. He added if the law school building were named for the person who was actually responsible for the building it would be called "Dorsett Hall." He was obviously referring to Tony Dorsett, the star football player at Pittsburgh, whose exploits on the football field helped raise enough money to pay for the building.

But a successful football program's benefit to the university cannot just be measured in dollars. Additionally one has to consider the number of students who are quicker to come to a university because of a successful football (or to a lesser extent, basketball) program. I have heard that the dean of one law school claimed the quality of his student applications rose by 25 percent after his university won the national championship in football.

One might be surprised to learn a law student would actually care about the success of a school's football team, but that ignores the high visibility of football. Students frequently want to attend a high visibility school. Plus, there may be the perception if the football team is good, so is the law school.

Despite what seems like an inflated salary, the life of a football coach is no bed of roses. Let's compare him to what at first blush seems like a grossly underpaid law professor. Apart from the fact that a law professor like me does not bring anywhere near the same level of revenue as a football coach, consider our relative levels of security. If I take a moot court team to a competition and they perform poorly, say lose in the first round, nothing bad will happen to me. Indeed, even if I say something on the pages of the A-J that my dean, provost, president or chancellor does not like, I cannot be fired because I have tenure.

On the other hand, let a football coach have a losing season, and what happens? Frequently, he is out of work. Even if he has done well in the past, many universities are going to want to know: "What have you done for me lately?" And, if the university doesn't like the answer, the coach may well find himself unemployed. So, while football coaches may enjoy what most of the rest of us consider exorbitant salaries, the pressure, importance to the university, and lack of job security justify those salaries.

Charles: Colleges collect cash; players get injured

I apologize to Texas Tech football coach Kliff Kingsbury in advance and make clear the disclaimer that I am a loyal Red Raider fan. That said, I take the position that major college football coaches are overpaid. The professor operates from a false assumption that the vast salaries paid to college football coaches are beneficial to the educational institutions they serve. He also overlooks important policy considerations that are extremely important in this debate.

Let's start with some numbers. The 535 coaches for men's sports collected a total of $440 million in salary and an average of $823,000 per full-time positions in 2014, as reported by CNN Money. This includes basketball coaches and other sports but is weighed heavily in favor of the big money winner: college football. Emblematic of this escalated pay scale is Nick Saban, coach of the University of Alabama, who makes $6.9 million, which is more than the salary paid to most NFL coaches. Add to the mix Ohio State's Urban Meyer ($4.6 million), Texas' Mack Brown (no longer coaching but made more than $5 million) and even Navy's Ken Niumatalolo ($1.5 million).

So, what's wrong with these high salaries? The professor argues that the big bucks paid to college football coaches is earned by the dollars brought in to the universities and status conferred thereon. Joe Nocera, in his opinion piece on this subject in the *New York Times*, got it right when he said the coaches are overpaid.

"At a time when state legislatures are cutting back their support for public universities," Nocera wrote, "when most big athletic programs lose money, when tuition has never been higher, there is something terribly askew about the skyrocketing compensation of college football (and men's basketball) coaches."

Professor Loewy might wish to revisit his underlying assumption the big money suck is a win-win for the coaches and universities.

On the flip side, this pay dynamic offers few benefits, if at all, to the college athletes and the students. According to CNN, "The head coaches in the five major athletic conferences earn more than their schools spend on all athletic scholarships combined." At the very least, these salaries should be trimmed or monies reallocated to provide greater scholarship and tuition support to the students who are facing mounting tuition and expenses, even at public universities.

A particularly unnerving effect of this wage disparity is the exploitation of student athletes, which is a hotly debated issue and a potential topic for another installment of this column. College athletes are exploited as commodities by the universities, which receive a massive outlay from television for broadcast rights. The athletes who put their very lives in jeopardy every time they play receive no compensation whatsoever. Keep in mind that while the vast majority of players will never see the consummation of an NFL player contract, they are exposed to life-crippling head injuries and other deleterious health consequences.

Let's face it, Professor Loewy, the inflated salaries paid to football coaches are not justified and work to the disadvantage of the institutions and students they serve.

Arnold: Most of money comes from happy alumni

Mr. Moster's most salient point is his totally correct observation that we live in "a time when legislatures are cutting back their support for public universities ..." That observation is completely correct, which, of course means that public universities must figure out another way to obtain money. The two sources most commonly used are tuition increases and alumni/booster contributions.

Obviously tuition increases can and should be limited if a university wishes to maintain its status as one that is truly public.

That leaves alumni and booster contribution. Of course, in an ideal world, a successful alumnus from the university would be overjoyed to contribute $20 million to the law school, science department or school of dramatic arts even if the football team went 1-11 the year before or the school doesn't even have a football team.

Undoubtedly such gifts do happen from time to time at places like Harvard or the University of Chicago, and I am quite sure occasionally at Texas Tech. But this is not the norm. Rather these contributions are usually correlated to football success. I can almost guarantee you that if our Red Raiders were to go 12-0 in football next year and beat Alabama in the national championship game, our alumni contributions would go through the roof, and the caliber of student who applies to the various component parts of the university will see a major increase.

Additionally, coaches' salaries and buyouts are frequently financed by alumni and other boosters. To the extent that this happens, not only are universities benefitted by the success of the football program in terms of gifts to the university's academic program, but frequently those same donors pay for all or part of the coach's salary.

Let's look at a couple of Mr. Moster's examples. First, Nick Saban of Alabama. Mr. Moster might actually understate Saban's salary. According to a recent *USA Today* article, the university board of trustees approved a contract of more than $11 million for Saban as part of a long-term contract that will pay him $65 million plus incentive bonuses through 2025.

Now, why would a presumably reasonable board of trustees think that this is a prudent investment. I see two reasons. First, the image he has created for the university is sufficient to attract large sums of money, more than what seems to be his inflated salary. Second, the improvement to the image of the university that his football team has created has in all probability increased the number and quality of prospective student applicants.

Let's now look at Mr. Moster's Mack Brown example. Brown had a long and distinguished career with the University of Texas during which he resurrected the Longhorns sagging football prominence, returning them to their past days of glory. However, after doing that, he had a couple of mediocre seasons whereupon some influential donors decided, wrongly as it turned out, the Longhorns needed a new leader and thus Brown was eased out—fired, if you prefer. While I shed no tears for Mr. Brown, who I am sure received a handsome severance settlement and a network job as a broadcaster, his case illustrates my point about the volatility of the job, which I as a tenured professor do not have to face.

One final point that Mr. Moster makes about which I do not disagree is that the student athletes should be better compensated than they are. I have debated this question on the pages of this newspaper with my colleague, Brian Shannon, our faculty athletic representative. With what I have said about how much universities benefit from successful football programs, it seems clear to me that a scholarship, while substantial and of great value, is not always sufficient to pay for the value that at least some student athletes add to the university's ability to raise itself.

Charles: Where is proof that winning helps colleges?

The professor agrees with my point that state legislatures are cutting back their support of public universities and yet continues to defend the bloated salaries paid to football coaches. Logically this view is unsupported in that many of these universities are still on the financial losing end even after taking into consideration ticket sales. Perhaps the professor would agree it is wrong for football coaches to be paid these high salaries when the net effect would result in a financial loss to the university?

Other points raised by the professor appear to be total conjecture unless he can come up with some hard figures. For example, he argues that "coaches' salaries and buyouts are frequently financed by alumni and other boosters." This unproven statement has no bearing on the critical issue as to whether such contributions are substantial enough to fill the financial void of a losing football program at a major university. He also asserts that a successful football program would benefit the applicable university by increasing "the number and quality of prospective student applicants." Sounds good, but where is the evidence of this? Conjecture does not serve the debate process and is certainly a recipe for losing a case in court.

Additionally, does the professor believe it is correct that the "head coaches of the five major athletic conferences earn more than their schools spend on all athletic scholarships combined?" Not only is that disparity deeply disturbing but I would further add funds be infused to the general student population for scholarships.

I am glad that the professor and I seem to be on the same page with regard to the unequal treatment of student athletes. I will go further by stating such treatment is abusive and tantamount to outright economic exploitation. It is outrageous these players are put in harm's way every time they play and receive absolutely no compensation from the universities they serve. There is a term that best describes their status as an exploited unpaid group, but I will leave it to our readers to fill in the blank.

College Coaches Are Overpaid

Joe Nocera

Joe Nocera is a Bloomberg Opinion columnist covering business. He has written business columns for Esquire, GQ, *and the* New York Times, *and is the former editorial director of* Fortune.

"Are Football Coaches Overpaid?" asks a new paper by two Vanderbilt University professors, Randall S. Thomas of the law school, and R. Lawrence Van Horn of the school of management. It's amazing the things academics can find worthy of study, isn't it?

My answer is: Of course they are. At a time when state legislatures are cutting back their support for public universities, when most big athletic programs lose money, when tuition has never been higher, there is something terribly askew about the skyrocketing compensation of college football (and men's basketball) coaches.

At the University of Alabama, Nick Saban makes a reported $6.9 million a year, more than most professional football coaches. At Ohio State, Urban Meyer makes $4.6 million. At the University of Texas, Mack Brown made more than $5 million before he resigned in December. Navy's football coach, Ken Niumatalolo, makes more than $1.5 million. Navy, no less!

But as my colleague Steve Eder reported in *The Times* this week, the Thomas and Van Horn paper comes to a very different conclusion. According to the paper, football coaches are not overpaid. Why not? Because their jobs—and their employment contracts—are very similar to those of chief executives.

"While university presidents are nominally the CEO of the university," they write, "there are many commentators, including some presidents, who believe that the football coach retains the role as the most powerful decision maker. Football coaches

"College Coaches Are Overpaid," by Joe Nocera, opinion columnist, *The New York Times*, September 5, 2014. Reprinted by permission.

have many of the same job characteristics as CEOs of public companies—they run large organizations with many employees that generate hundreds of millions of dollars in revenues."

The idea that football coaches, who run programs made up of maybe 200 people and generating at most $100 million (and that's at the top) are comparable to public university presidents with budgets of $2 billion is just silly. But there is something apt about comparing them to chief executives. After all, in the land of the overpaid, chief executives are at the top of the heap.

The justification for outlandish executive compensation is that chief executives are being rewarded for performance. But it doesn't always work that way. In truth, far too many corporate chieftains take home millions of dollars each year whether their companies perform well or not. It's a rigged game: The board that sets chief executive pay is often made up of other CEOs, who are deeply sympathetic to the man whose pay they are setting. Performance measures can be changed to make the chief executive look good. And so on.

Thomas and Van Horn make the point that it is much easier to measure the performance of a college football coach—he either wins games or he doesn't. The average tenure of a Division I football coach, they report, is just three years, so the coach has every incentive to maximize his earnings. That may indeed explain why football coaches seek bigger salaries, but it doesn't explain why they are getting them.

There are really two reasons, one of which Thomas and Van Horn mention and the other of which they don't. The one they mention is television money, which has flooded into college sports in recent years. They point out that after the Pac-12 Conference negotiated an expansive TV deal in 2011—nearly quadrupling television revenue for some teams in the conference—Washington State was able to pay its new football coach $2.25 million, up from $600,000. "A windfall," one athletic director calls it.

What they don't mention is that other than facilities, travel costs and coaches' salaries, there aren't many other places to spend the money. The players don't get paid, but the money has to go somewhere. So the coaches grab the lion's share. Economists call this rent-seeking behavior.

In the recent O'Bannon decision, the judge ruled that universities would have to up the value of their athletic scholarships to cover the full cost of attendance. In most cases, that means an increase of between $1,000 to $3,000 per scholarship.

Not long ago, the *News & Observer* of Raleigh, N.C., interviewed Bubba Cunningham, the athletic director at the University of North Carolina, about his concerns in the wake of the O'Bannon decision. Cunningham estimated that adding on the full cost of attendance would cost his university $1.8 million. At UNC the football coach, Larry Fedora, makes around $1.7 million. The basketball coach, Roy Williams, makes a little over $1.8 million.

"We don't have $1.8 million discretionary," he said, referring to the full cost of attendance. "That's going to create challenges." He suggested that certain minor sports might be "at risk." But he also said that certain other options "aren't realistic."

"Like what?" asked the interviewer.

"Slowing down facility expansion, or salaries," he replied.

Which is the final way CEO compensation resembles the pay of college football coaches: It never goes down.

The NCAA Fails to Hold Coaches Accountable

Joseph Cooper and Jasmine Harris

Joseph Cooper is assistant professor of educational leadership at the University of Connecticut. His research focuses on the nexus between sport, education, race, and culture with an emphasis on sport as a catalyst for holistic development and positive changes in society. Jasmine Harris is assistant professor of sociology at Ursinus College. Her research focuses on institutional racism and misogyny in the academy and entrepreneurship in the Black community.

Maryland college football coach DJ Durkin was ultimately fired after the death of a player during practice—and findings that his players were bullied and abused by coaches and staff over the course of his three-year tenure. However, his 11th hour ouster on Oct. 31 is evidence of how much the culture of college football still needs to change.

This culture encourages players to ignore signs of physical or mental exhaustion and is present across the college football landscape, not just at Maryland.

Durkin may be gone, but only because the public—including current players, students and alumni at the University of Maryland—wanted him gone. It wasn't because the people in charge of Maryland's university system suddenly realized how wrong it was for Durkin to run a program in which complaining of pain was seen as unmanly.

The board of regents at the University System of Maryland actually wanted to keep Durkin. The board even reportedly pressured University of Maryland President Wallace Loh to keep Durkin or risk losing his own job.

Loh initially responded by announcing his own resignation. But after hearing the public outcry after the board moved to reinstate Durkin—Loh fired Durkin instead.

In a statement, Loh noted how "the overwhelming majority of stakeholders expressed serious concerns about Coach DJ Durkin returning to the campus."

"This is a difficult decision, but it is the right one for our entire University," Loh stated. He also vowed to devote the remaining months of his presidency to "advancing the needed reforms in our Athletic Department that prioritize the safety and well-being of our student-athletes."

A student-led protest was reportedly being planned before the firing took place.

In our view as researchers who focus on the intersection of race and college sports, none of these events will rid big-time college sports of its deepest problems. Those problems include the placing of winning games and generating revenue ahead of the best interests of the student-athletes.

In recent years, legal activists like former athletes Ed O'Bannon, Cain Colter and Martin Jenkins have sought to change this state of affairs.

Risking Their Lives

It would be naive not to view big-time college sports through the lens of race. A recent report that shows black males make up only 2.4 percent of the general student body at Power 5 Bowl Championship Series schools, but 55 percent and 56 percent, respectively, of football and men's basketball teams.

Further, black male college athletes graduate at the lowest rates among all college athletes and in the NCAA and Division I Power 5 member institutions, which generate billions of dollars primarily off the broadcasting and sponsorship rights for football and men's basketball.

These trends underscore how black males are primarily valued at these institutions as athletic gladiators, but not as students deserving of quality educational opportunities and support for their overall well-being.

Failed to Render Medical Aid

Had Durkin been allowed to continue to coach despite the toxic culture uncovered at Maryland following the May 2018 death of 19-year-old offensive lineman Jordan McNair, many would have considered it a gross miscarriage of justice.

McNair died of heatstroke during practice earlier this year. A cold-water immersion would have likely saved his life but team staff and coaches failed to promptly seek medical assistance.

While player deaths during practice may be rare, indifference toward black athletes, especially their physical and mental health, is widespread in college sports.

The prevalence of college athletes' unmet mental and physical health needs is well-documented. The NCAA's Sport Science Institute, through its own research, has acknowledged that college athletes' health issues remain a major problem.

Disparities in Discipline?

Yet, as the story of Durkin demonstrates, both the NCAA—and the University of Maryland as one of its member institutions—have failed to create and enforce policies that hold coaches responsible for creating conditions that are injurious to college athletes' overall well-being.

The system seems more bent on policing and punishing black student-athletes than it does on holding accountable those who are responsible for their care.

For instance, several players on the University of North Carolina football team were suspended for four games for selling their team-issued shoes in violation of NCAA rules. Another black player, a University of Central Florida kicker, was ruled ineligible after receiving money through a YouTube channel he created.

These student-athletes who engaged in victimless acts and tried to make a few dollars in a system that makes billions of dollars from their labor are made to sit out games or get kicked off the team entirely. Yet, as demonstrated by the initial decision to keep Durkin, neglecting the health needs of a player in medical distress is excusable.

Balancing Academics and Sports

Being a college athlete is inherently tough work. One of us is conducting research into black Division I football and men's basketball players. Thus far, the research shows 64 percent of respondents find it difficult or very difficult to balance their student and athlete identities while they're in season, compared to only 34 percent when out of season.

These numbers illustrate the imbalance in what college athletes are expected to do versus how much time they have for school. If it's already difficult for players to manage the demands of college and the obligations to their team, how much more difficult was it for Maryland football players, who faced a football culture that normalized physical and mental abuse under Durkin. It was noted in a report that before McNair passed away, one of the staff called him a vulgar name for a female private part.

College football players are not allowed to form a union. In our view, this curtails their ability to seek recourse if their rights are being violated.

Before Durkin was fired, blame initially fell on strength and conditioning coach Rick Court, who resigned after McNair's death. Court was, in some ways, cast as a bad apple and the tragedy allowed to be seen as an isolated case of inattentiveness to one player's medical needs by a few replaceable athletic staff.

The Wrong Kind of Firing

It's important to note that in being "fired," Durkin is still reportedly being bought out for the remainder of his five-year contract, valued at more than $5 million.

If the University of Maryland had taken the more difficult route of firing Durkin for just cause and taking away his payout, that would have sent a powerful message that players' lives matter.

College Coaches Have Many Responsibilities

S. R. Johnson, P. J. Wojnar, W. J. Price, T. J. Foley, J. R. Moon, E. N. Esposito, and F. J. Cromartie

Scott Johnson is the chair of sports coaching at the United States Sports Academy. All contributing authors are residential faculty members at the United States Sports Academy.

Since the beginning of sport competition, athletes have sought to acquire the skills and knowledge of sport in order to become "champions." As sport evolved into organized activity, coaches began working more closely with athletes on sport skill development. Education and training programs have been created, over the past 30 years, in an effort to assist coaches and athletes with the development of methods and strategies for achieving peak performance. When designing a coaching education program, however, one must ask what do coaches need to know; what are the essential elements of athletic coaching?

In the 1960s, Dr. Thomas P. Rosandich, founder of the United States Sports Academy, outlined what he called the American Training Patterns (personal communication, April 2010), which focused on physical components of training; namely, speed, skill, stamina, strength, and suppleness (i.e., flexibility). Over time, our knowledge of how to train these five components has become more comprehensive and has been expanded into other disciplines as coaches continue striving to develop exceptional athletes (i.e., "champions"). Though early emphasis in coaching focused on athletic performance enhancement and basic physiology, other disciplines of human performance eventually became components of

"A Coach's Responsibility: Learning How to Prepare Athletes for Peak Performance," by Scott R. Johnson, Pamela J. Wojnar, William J. Price, Timothy J. Foley, Jordan R. Moon, Enrico N. Esposito, and Fred J. Cromartie, United States Sports Academy. Reprinted by permission.

training athletes. The purpose of this article is to examine the aforementioned components and introduce the world to the United States Sports Academy's newly revised American Coaching Patterns.

American Coaching Patterns is a six-course program, encompassing six fundamentals of training: stamina, strength, suppleness or flexibility, agility, speed and skill. The six courses focus on sports administration, coaching methods, sports medicine, strength and conditioning, sports psychology, and athlete development. With the addition of these new disciplines, training athletes has become a holistic activity focusing on the entire athlete (i.e., mental and physical aspects).

Risk Management

Participating in sports involves a certain level of risk, even when reasonable precautions have been implemented. Coaches have some level of responsibility for all aspects of their athletic program. For example, coaches need to be concerned about the welfare of their players and the maintenance of athletic equipment and facilities. These responsibilities fall under the umbrella of risk management and the controlled evaluation of the athletic environment. Evaluating risk management in the athletic environment is a significant administrative element for coaches. While risk can never be fully eliminated, these individuals must be aware of, and must seek to limit the chances liability exposure. Hence, coaches must exert significant effort to monitor all components of their athletic programs.

Coaches must realize they will encounter facility and/or equipment risk on a constant basis. A substantial amount of time is required to assess sport facilities and equipment in order to prevent injury to sport participants during competition. Numerous sport facilities continue to be built in order to house athletic competitions making facility risk management a top priority of coaches. In order to create a regular routine that will lead to a safe environment, coaches should follow five guidelines set by Dougherty and Bonanno: 1) implement regular inspection and maintenance of schedules for facilities and equipment used, 2) ensure that facilities exceed regulatory safety standards, 3) ensure that equipment used exceeds regulatory safety standards, 4) ensure that the installing of new equipment is completed by a professional, and 5) ensure that all equipment used is safe and appropriate for the participants involved in the sport activity.

Several risk management measures can be employed by coaches in order to minimize external risks. Examples include reviewing sport participants' insurance coverage twice per year, reporting sport-related incidents in a timely manner to proper authorities (e.g., insurance companies, medical personnel), identifying potential hazards to the proper authorities (e.g., facility management), and confirming sport participants have obtained medical examinations and authorization to play. Even though peak athletic performance (e.g., wins and losses) can become a focal point for coaches, attention to detail and organization are primary responsibilities when attempting to decrease the potential negative impact of external risks on an athletic program.

Therefore, coaches should be aware of the factors associated with risk management. Coaches can limit the amount of risk involved with their programs by implementing effective management processes and staying up-to-date on changes occurring in the external environment. It is important for coaches to have a positive outlook concerning the future of their programs. In order to gain additional knowledge and remain current with issues concerning risk management, coaches should review literature published by their school or university, athletic associations, or national sport governing bodies regularly. This will help coaches minimize external risks while preparing their athletes for competition which is critical for the development of a successful program.

Injury Prevention

According to the National Federation of State High School Associations, an estimated 7.6 million individuals in the United States participated in high school sports during 2009–10. These participation rates are a cause for hope that the increasing effort to get adolescents to be physically active can be successful. Unfortunately, competing in athletics increases the opportunity to experience a sport injury. The Centers for Disease Control and Prevention indicated more than 1.4 million injuries occurred in high school sport participants during the 2005-06 school year.

Therefore, coaches should gain knowledge concerning first aid care and the prevention of injury. When coaches teach their athletes sport skills, these athletes must develop precise technical movements in order to produce peak athletic performance. Such movements, along with the demands placed on athletes' muscles when accelerating, decelerating, or changing direction, increase the risk of injury. These performance demands create internal forces on athletes' bodies and when combined with external forces (e.g., body contact), injury risk can significantly increase. Coaches need to be aware of these potential risks when developing training regimens for participants competing at any level of sport.

Today, young athletes train like elite professional athletes. Specifically, many adolescents are undertaking physical and mental conditioning regimens for several hours a day in order to produce peak athletic performance. Additionally, some individuals are specializing in one sport at an early age and participating on several teams during a single athletic season. While others participate in several different sports year-round (without allowing the body and mind enough time to sufficiently recover from the rigors of athletic competition.

Thus, sport participation and demanding athletic training regimens can produce significant sport injuries for athletes.

Experiencing a sport injury may affect an athlete physically and psychologically once the individual returns to athletic competition. Without question, coaches should realize athletes need athletic healthcare. In addition, this healthcare should be considered an investment toward individuals maintaining a physically active lifestyle in the future.

Proper management only comes from being prepared and trained on how to respond prudently to a situation. Coaches and medical personnel (e.g., athletic trainers) must provide a safe environment for sport participation and be prepared to respond when an injury occurs. In order to accomplish these objectives, communication among all individuals associated with sport participation must be accomplished. "Coaches are key members of the sports medicine team and have a great deal of interaction with ATCs (i.e., certified athletic trainers) at all levels of competition."

Communication

Besides interacting with medical personnel, coaches must be exceptional communicators with their athletes in order to be effective teachers. The ability to communicate is a critical component in becoming a successful coach and developing elite athletes. "Communication is a process through which two entities exchange formal messages in a common code by using one or more transmission channels …" It is the foundation upon which coaches build their team. Coaching without effective communication is like trying to play basketball without a ball; it just is not a successful endeavor. "In fact, effective communication is often cited as a critical element in the success of athletic teams." Team members must learn how to communicate with each other both in and out of the playing arena so that they can become one cohesive unit and ultimately increase their level of success.

Coaches can be extremely knowledgeable in the technical skills of the sport and have the perfect game plan; but if they cannot communicate this information to their team, the likelihood of a victory will be greatly reduced. Sullivan indicated "there is a positive correlation between enhanced interpersonal communication skills and higher levels of team performance." An athlete and coach speak the common language of the specific sport in which they are involved, but "the communication must be articulated in a fashion that the athletes will not only hear, but also instantly understand." Joe Torre, former Major League Baseball manager who led the New York Yankees to four World Series titles, emphasized that "communication is the key to trust, and trust is the key to teamwork in any group endeavor, be it in sports, business, or family."

Coaches have the opportunity to teach their players many life skills and effective communication may be the most valuable one, yet time is not always in the coach's favor. From limits on practice time or set times for half-time and timeouts during athletic competition, coaches encounter several constraints which can limit the time allowed to convey messages to their players. Therefore, coaches should organize their messages efficiently in hopes of developing positive relationships with players. Without question, establishing a positive athlete-coach relationship is a critical component to achieving effective communication between these individuals. Communicating effectively will allow coaches to teach their athletes the necessary sport skills to produce peak performance and increase the possibility of having a successful athletic program.

No relationship, whether on the playing field or off, can blossom without communication and the relationship between players and coaches is no different. Players need to feel that their coach cares about them as a person; not just as an athlete who can help them win games and establish a successful athletic program. Players are people first and great coaches make time for the person as well as the player.

"You could go into the coach's office and he would be all ears." This helped to create an atmosphere that was comfortable for the athletes: "You never felt like you were stepping over a boundary if you were to walk into their office and ask them a question."

Being available to athletes and other team personnel is only as effective as the communication that takes place. Coaches must remember that communication is a two-way street; it requires listening as well as talking because it involves both inputs and outputs. If managed effectively and by making an effort to develop positive relationships with their players, coaches can increase the chances of team success.

Whether it's the end of a close game, during practice, or at a meeting unrelated to the team or even the sport, it is incumbent on the coach to create an environment that fosters communication. "Effective communication is apparent when team members listen to one another and attempt to build on each other's contributions." Coaches should incorporate communication into every practice because it is one of the fundamentals of sport.

Nutrition

As coaches establish a positive relationship with their athletes, many athletes begin to realize the importance of training the body physically in order to produce peak performances. Hence, every coach should consider performance enhancement to be the number one priority when developing a strength and conditioning program. However, without adequate nutrition, training results may be suboptimal due to a lack of recovery and reduced ability to perform due to depleted energy. Therefore, nutrition is the foundation of performance enhancement. Without optimal nutrition, athletes cannot compete to their full potential.

Over the last few decades the nutritional requirements of athletes have been researched extensively. Sports nutrition has come a long way from the "take a salt tablet" days. We now understand the importance of specific nutrients and when and how they need to be ingested, as well as how much should be consumed. A good place to start is the standard food guide pyramid. While the pyramid as we know it has been modified over the last decade, the principles of a well-balanced diet remain the same. For an athlete, these principles still apply; however, they need to be modified based on the sport and type of athlete and the intensity of his training.

Water is also a key nutritional component for athletes. It is recommended that six to eight ounces of water be consumed every five to 15 minutes during exercise. Athletes should not rely on thirst as an indicator of when to drink water, and coaches should not restrict water as punishment, as this could lead to a reduction in performance and possible serious health consequences. In an effort to stay hydrated athletes can weigh themselves before and after physical activity. Based on every pound lost, the athlete should consume three cups of water. Additionally, coaches need to be aware of environmental conditions that can increase the rate of dehydration, such as hot and humid environments, and schedule water breaks at specific times during practice.

Key nutrients that need to be increased for all athletes include carbohydrates (e.g., bread, oats, and grains) and proteins (e.g., meat, nuts, and dairy). Intense exercise significantly depletes the body of stored carbohydrates and causes significant muscle damage. Coaches need to ensure athletes consume extra carbohydrates and protein after completing intense physical activity. Extra carbohydrates replace the lost carbohydrates stored in the body and drive cellular activity for repair. Protein helps muscles repair and grow. Increasing protein intake to between 1.4 and 2.0 g/kg of body weight per day is suggested for both endurance and strength athletes, while carbohydrates should be increased to as much as eight to 10 g/kg of body weight per day. Often, an athlete's diet consists of 55-65% carbohydrates, 10 to 15% protein, and 25-35% fat. These percentages are often modified based on the sport and body type of the athlete. Using grams per kilogram of body weight to develop a nutritional plan for an athlete is ideal. Athletes need to eat well-balanced meals and to supplement with additional proteins (i.e., powders/ drinks) and carbohydrates (i.e., sugary drink such as Gatorade/ Powerade) only when they are not reaching the minimum requirements in their regular diet. Supplementing with vitamins and minerals may be needed for some athletes with specific nutritional needs, such as vegans. Nutrient timing also plays an important role during training and should be practiced by coaches wishing to optimize training results and promote recovery. Specifically, carbohydrates and protein need to be consumed immediately after exercise.

Performance enhancing supplements also need to be considered when discussing the nutritional needs of athletes. Three ergogenic aids that are recommended for athletes include caffeine, creatine, and beta-alanine. These supplements work through specific physiological mechanisms that can improve performance. However, coaches need to be educated about these products before making recommendations to athletes. Several articles have been published indicating proper dosage and the specific benefits for each substance and can be accessed for free on the Internet.

Understanding nutrition is a start towards reaching optimal performance. Multiple factors can influence overall performance; however, starting with the basics, such as nutrition, can lead to greater improvements in performance regardless of the training program. Utilizing an ideal training program while implementing a proper nutritional program will enable athletes to realize optimal enhancements in performance.

Goal Setting

When completing a strength and conditioning program, a coach may instruct an athlete to complete "another repetition." Coaches have a responsibility to prepare their athletes physically and mentally for athletic competition. Thus, many athletes develop a desire to produce successful performance and gain mastery of any task completed. For example, an athlete may not only want to win the contest but may also aspire to perform sport skills exceptionally well in order to produce peak performance. Without question, coaches have an opportunity to assist athletes with performance enhancement.

Locke and Latham explained that an individual's level of success in athletic competition is primarily dependent upon skill and motivation. Therefore, a primary responsibility of coaches is to motivate their athletes to perform at optimal levels. Sage indicated motivation is the direction and intensity of an individual's effort.

Some coaches use motivational techniques when establishing their athletes' training regimens. One technique, which has been used to promote commitment, perseverance, dedication, and effort to create an individual's long-term self-motivation is goal setting. An objective goal refers to "attaining a specific standard of proficiency on a task, usually within a specified time"; while a subjective goal (e.g., I want to enjoy playing in the game) can be vague and difficult for coaches and athletes to measure.

As Locke and Latham stated, practitioners and researchers have examined empirical research concerning goal setting for almost four decades. During this time, Locke and Latham developed a goal setting theory that is well established on the review of approximately 400 laboratory and field research investigations. Even though a majority of these investigations occurred in industrial/organizational psychology, "goal setting can be used effectively on any domain in which an individual or group has some control over the outcomes." Goal setting investigations examining Locke and Latham's theory have occurred in sports settings. Results indicate assigned specific, difficult goals (i.e., hard goals) lead to a higher level of performance in comparison to easy and vague goals (i.e., "do your best"). Interestingly, a positive, linear relation between goal difficulty and performance is evident when an individual is committed to the goal, has developed the ability (i.e., talent) to attain the goal, and no conflicting goals are present.

As a positive athlete-coach relationship develops, many athletes begin considering their coaches to be role models. Hence, coaches should communicate with their athletes in order to assist them with the development of personal goals. An athlete's personal goals can lead to skill development and ultimately peak performance. In a professional manner, a coach may provide an athlete with constructive feedback concerning skill development, safety, nutrition, or injury prevention. Thus, an athlete can use this communication to establish a personal SMART goal which is specific, measurable, attainable, realistic, and time-bound; such as, reducing one's running time to complete a 5K race by 15 seconds within the next 12 months. The formation of SMART goals can provide an athlete with the motivation and commitment to yield athletic success.

Coaches need to be aware athletes should develop a series of short-term goals which allow measurable progress toward achieving a long-term goal. Using the previous SMART goal (i.e., reducing one's running time to complete a 5K race by 15 seconds within the next 12 months) as a "long-term" goal, a coach can communicate with an athlete to create short-term goals. For example, one may create a goal to reduce running time to complete a 5K race by 5 seconds within the next 4 months. After four months, a coach can assist the athlete with evaluating athletic performance and determine if the short-term goal was accomplished. If the goal is accomplished, establish another short-term SMART goal. If the goal is not achieved, reevaluate the athlete's performance and assist with developing another short-term SMART goal. Make certain the athlete possesses the skill and motivation to successfully pursue the established long-term SMART goal.

Coaches should also realize group goal setting may be an effective strategy for enhancing group performance in sport and physical activity. For example, members of a team may establish a goal to score at least 50 points per game for the next four weeks. As goal setting research continues, Locke and Latham's goal setting theory can provide coaches with additional knowledge concerning individual and group performance enhancement.

How Coaches Should Apply This Information

As described in previous sections, coaching education includes knowledge from several disciplines. The nature of a coach's job is affected by the athlete's stage of development. This will determine what kind of knowledge the coach needs and how it will be applied. The final piece of the coaching puzzle centers on how to make the coaching process athlete centered. No matter what the specific training discipline, a coach needs to understand the stages of athletic development in addition to knowledge of how individuals grow and mature.

Training Stages

Athletes progress through several training stages as they get older and become more accomplished in their sport. For the most part training stages are age related. Each stage's curriculum should help athletes transition to the next stage by providing what they will need at their present training stage as well as preparing them for the proceeding one.

Training stages also take advantage of periods of accelerated adaptation for various training components. For example, significant increases in aerobic capacity occur after the onset of peak height velocity so aerobic training should take priority during this period which generally lasts for 12 to 18 months. The accelerated period for learning skills occurs from about 8 to 11 years of age for girls and 9 to 12 years of age for boys, so during this period it makes sense to focus on skill development. Speed has two periods of accelerated adaptation, one as a result of changes in the central nervous system (6 to 9 years of age), and the other resulting from changes due to training stimuli (11 to 13 years of age for girls and 13 to 16 years of age for boys). By periodizing on a career scale, coaches can take advantage of these various periods and be assured that athletes are being provided with training appropriate with developmental goals.

Early vs. Late Maturing Athletes

Most countries use an athlete development system that focuses on performance outcomes. This involves getting as many young athletes as possible into training programs and then focusing on the elite performers. The problem with this method is that sport governing bodies rely on early maturing youngsters—those who are simply bigger and stronger than their peers and who, almost inevitably, perform better in sport. However, only an estimated 25% of youngsters identified as "elite athletes" at an early age were identified the same way at a later date; indicating late maturers can also become "elite athletes" if given enough time to develop.

The outcome model tends to quickly discard those who do not measure up, and while this may not be by design it happens often enough to be considered a characteristic of the model itself. In the outcome model young athletes are treated as small adults, following the same training and competition patterns as older athletes. Late maturers are discouraged from continued sport participation since the outcome model rewards early maturers with more coach contact, encouragement, and social recognition due to their early ability (i.e., athletic-talent).

A better model might focus on the process of developing an athlete. This model is more inclusive because the path from instruction, to training, and finally, to competition is paved with intentionally stage-appropriate activities and training. Early maturing or physically precocious youngsters do not affect this model. In a process model, stages of physical and athletic development are paired so that athletes are receiving the instruction and training they need at times when it is most beneficial. By deliberately focusing on process rather than outcome providers of youth sport will be able to keep youngsters involved in programs for longer periods. Over the long term this will help athletes develop an appreciation for physical activity and sport. It will also help sport governing bodies reduce the early vs. late maturer problem.

By making a conscious effort to keep all athletes involved through stage-appropriate modifications in training and competition, sport governing bodies will provide a better sport experience for everyone and increase the likelihood of developing elite athletes from those who might otherwise have dropped out from participating in sport. Not only will this enlarge the pool of talent available to national sport governing bodies but it will also increase the likelihood that athletes will continue to be physically active throughout life. Specifically, as youths progress into adulthood, these individuals will have the competence to use skills and knowledge they acquired in organized sports to remain healthy and physically fit.

Burnout and Dropout

The terms "burnout" and "dropout" are frequently used as if they mean the same thing. However, burnout refers to the long-term effects of overtraining or inappropriate training based on the age of the athlete. Symptoms of burnout are frequent or chronic injury, lack of progress in training and competition, and general dissatisfaction with the sport; the key component is long-term involvement in training programs. Dropout refers to the phenomena of athletes simply quitting their sport participation prematurely. Coaches should realize dropout is more detrimental to the athlete and the sport governing body. Following accepted athlete development guidelines and constructing career periodization plans which adhere to these guidelines, coaches can reduce both dropout and burnout.

In 2008 over 44 million youth participated in youth sport activities throughout the United States. Although this is an increase of over 6 million participants since the National Council of Youth Sports report in 2000 it is estimated that 35% of youth involved in such athletic programs drop out each year. Since millions of young athletes participate in adult organized and supervised activities coaches must gain a solid understanding of performance enhancement and proper coaching methods. By providing a better sport experience for all participants more children will have the skills and knowledge needed to participate in life-long activity. Maintaining a physically-active lifestyle may help alleviate present-day mental and physical health issues associated with youth obesity.

Conclusion

Ultimately, coaches should be passionate about teaching sport skills to their athletes. Coaches must be life-long learners of sport in order to properly train their athletes for peak performance. As the profession of sport coaching has evolved and sport has become a multi-billion dollar industry, many coaches have discovered sport incorporates both physical and mental training. Therefore, in today's sports world, several disciplines have been integrated into the science and art of training athletes.

Based on the guidance and leadership of Dr. Thomas P. Rosandich, the United States Sports Academy has created the

American Coaching Patterns; a six-course program, embracing six basic fundamentals of training: stamina, strength, flexibility, agility, speed, and skill. This article presented information that coaches should utilize when training their athletes. These six courses, which comprise the American Coaching Patterns, emphasize sports administration, coaching methods, sports medicine, strength and conditioning, sports psychology, and athlete development. Training athletes to become "champions" in sport, and more importantly life, can provide many individuals with opportunities to produce peak performance.

Coaches' Compensations Reflect Their Value to Their Schools

Jasmine Harris

Jasmine Harris is director of the African American Studies program at the University of Texas, San Antonio. Her research focuses on institutional racism and misogyny in the academy and entrepreneurship in the Black community.

As college football bowl and playoff games unfold before a TV audience of millions, most of the attention will be on the final scores. Less is likely to be said about certain bonuses that the coaches get for their bowl and playoff appearances.

For instance, when the Fresno State Bulldogs defeated Arizona State in the Las Vegas Bowl on Dec. 15, the Bulldogs' coach, Jeff Tedford, already being paid US$1.6 million per year through 2021, got a $200,000 bonus for the win. He would have gotten $100,000 even if his team had lost.

Western Michigan's Tim Lester gets $25,000 for making it to the Famous Idaho Potato Bowl on Dec. 21.

Since college football coaches are already often the highest-paid public employees in their state—their eye-popping salaries often dwarfing even those of state governors—it may seem strange that coaches could collect bonuses that surpass most families' annual income, on top of it all.

It may also be tempting to think of the bonuses as being a byproduct of lucrative marketing deals that colleges started to get in the 1980s and television contracts that they started to get in the 1990s. But history shows that bonuses for college football coaches stretch back to the early 1900s, well before the invention of television or even the first commercial radio broadcast.

These bonuses create a market for winning that fuels the business of college sports. In my view as a scholar who studies big-time college football, these bonuses are not a reaction to a multi-billion-dollar market that rewards winning—they are the foundation of it.

Bonuses Go Back to Early 1900s

The first superstar college football coach contract on record to include compensation beyond base salary was signed by the legendary John Heisman—for whom the coveted Heisman Trophy is named—to coach Georgia Tech's football team in 1904.

Records show that Heisman's contract added 30 percent of all ticket sales to his annual $2,500, a salary that would have been the equivalent of just under $71,000 in 2018 dollars.

Heisman's contract was an acknowledgment that the football coach was uniquely intertwined with revenue generated during games. But it was also notable, as coaches' salaries were then often decided based on the relationship to faculty and administrator salaries. Ewald Stiehm, University of Nebraska head football coach from 1911 to 1915, was famously denied a $750 raise by the school because they didn't want a coach making more than the top professor. His salary at Nebraska was $4,250. He went to Indiana, which paid him $4,500.

Before television deals and marketing contracts, high salaries and added incentives were reserved for those top-tier coaches deemed capable of bringing a "winning culture" to the institution. Bear Bryant's 1954 contract was one of the few before 1980 to rival Heisman's. It included 1 percent of Texas A&M football ticket sales. Tickets in 1958 went for $3.50 per ticket.

Million-Dollar Men

The first million-dollar contract was signed by Bobby Bowden with Florida State University in 1995. Bowden only had one losing season in his 34 years at FSU and was coming off a 1993 National Championship when his contract was extended with a $300,000 per year raise, including another $700,000 in television appearance and apparel promotion bonuses. For the first time, pay was tied not just to winning—but to winning enough and in the right way. Exponential increases in revenue generated via ticket and apparel sales, bowl appearance payouts and even application pools beyond student athletes, are evidence of the value of wins—first culturally to university communities, then economically for universities' financial health.

A Bonus Bonanza

Today a long list of bonuses are included in contract offers to top coaches as additional compensation for winning.

Beyond incentives like home loans, car allowances and country club memberships, merit bonuses attached to bowl appearances, win-loss records, divisional rankings and national championships emphasize the value of coaches to their institutions. Some bonuses have little to do with the game's final score—like UConn's Randy Edsell earning a $2,000 bonus every time his football team scores first or leads at halftime.

The bonus money coaches are paid in exchange for those highly valued wins is a small fraction of what the institution earns for those wins. National tournament qualification and bowl appearances trigger additional bonuses, not only because they excite the fans but because they mean more revenue for the institution. Merit bonuses are a small price to pay to keep money flowing into a university through victories on the field—wins.

Cashing In

In my opinion, coaches aren't taking advantage of universities under this scheme. The universities are in on the joke. Universities were heavily involved in creating fiscal environments where high salaries and merit bonuses for coaches were more feasible. Bowden's 1995 contract would've been impossible if not for important legal victories led by individual universities seeking to transform college sports to big business.

For instance, the 1984 Supreme Court ruling in *NCAA v. Board of Regents of the University of Oklahoma* found in favor of individual universities negotiating television contracts directly with major networks. The ruling described the NCAA's control as in violation of anti-trust law. The move forever changed the financial landscape of college football and basketball, and introduced an influx of cash into the market.

The 1984 ruling meant schools and division conferences, like the Southeastern Conference, of which schools are members, could negotiate deals independent of the NCAA. The resulting influx of money into college football is directly connected to today's high coaches salaries. In 2017, when the Big Ten's new television deals with cable news networks ESPN and Fox kicked in, the conference was also home to five of the top 14 highest paid football coaches in the NCAA.

The Win-First Mentality

"Winning cultures" also encourage student athletes to buy into win-first, team-first thinking. This can be dangerous because it encourages coaches to push players beyond their limits. Earlier this year, University of Maryland football player Jordan McNair's death uncovered a record of dangerous workouts driven by then-head coach DJ Durkin and the university leadership's desire for wins and a stronger financial future.

The power given to coaches with winning records is not new. They are the foundation of college football. Before players or fans, there are coaches. As long as millions of people continue to enjoy college football games and attach so much meaning to the final score, football coaches will continue to fatten their pockets as a result.

Chapter 3

Is the Move to Superconferences Good for College Sports?

Overview: There Are Ways to Make College Athletics More Equitable

Andrew Bucholtz

Andrew Bucholtz is a staff writer for Awful Announcing and The Comeback. He previously worked at Yahoo! Sports Canada and Black Press.

One of the most unique things about college sports is the schools themselves have the power to remake their environment, and that's led to the chaotic round of conference realignment we've seen lately. The recent decisions by Nebraska and Colorado to leave the Big 12 for the Big 10 and the Pac-12 respectively, while noteworthy in their own right, may be just the first chips to fall in a round of conference realignment that could remake college football as we know it.

Texas A&M is well on the way to leaving the weakened Big 12 for the Southeastern Conference, and that could set off a round of dominos leading to 16-team superconferences. The key question for college football, though, is if that's really a good thing.

On the surface, larger conferences stacked with powerhouse programs have several points in their favor. For one thing, that could destroy the BCS and lead to a playoff system, such as the one recently outlined for *Forbes* by Webster University economics professor Dr. Patrick Rishe. A playoff could be imposed without superconferences, but the current lineup of six theoretically-equal (but far from practically-equal) BCS automatic qualification conferences and five non-automatic qualifying conferences makes it more difficult to come up with a fair set of entrance criteria.

If you have four 16-team superconferences, that's more likely to give you four deserving champions to receive automatic bid slots, and it gives you four at-large spots for independents, non-

"The Pros and Cons of NCAA Superconferences," by Andrew Bucholtz, The Good Point, September 15, 2011. Reprinted by permission.

superconference teams or superconference teams that don't win the conference championship. Under Rishe's system, most teams play no more games than they currently do; two of the four teams that win quarterfinals play one extra game (semifinals), while the other two play two extra games (semifinals and the national championship). This looks like a practical system, one that could generate extra money and interest, and one that would be easy to implement if superconferences came along.

Another benefit of superconferences is that they could do away with some of the despised non-conference cupcake games currently in existence. Larger conferences don't necessarily mean more conference games, but they could, and there would likely be less opposition to further conference games if there was an ironclad playoff berth for the conference champion instead of pressure to pad the resume with easy teams, go undefeated and lock up one of the two slots in the championship game. Most teams play eight conference games at the moment out of a 12-game schedule; boosting that to 10 or higher would make for substantially more compelling viewing week-in and week-out by eliminating some of the walkovers against cannon fodder, while still allowing for teams to play interesting non-conference clashes against other power teams.

However, there are significant perils associated with the superconference idea as well. Dallas Mavericks' owner and long-time NCAA playoff proponent Mark Cuban made some interesting points against the idea, most notably arguing that many schools would hate the eventual consequences of larger conferences; it's easy to get stuck in the basement of a big conference, and much tougher for occasionally strong schools to make a run when they've got multiple powerhouses to get past instead of just one or two.

There would also be less titles out there for the taking, too; a school like Connecticut that won the Big East football title in 2010 despite a less-than-stellar team might never be able to claim a title if they were in a larger conference; then again, they might never even make it into a bigger conference.

There are potential problems that go beyond football, too. If they come into existence, 16-team superconferences would certainly pose issues for many schools' other sports, and they might even result in the destruction and replacement of the NCAA basketball tournament.

Superconferences could also further increase the already-growing divisions between the big wealthy and powerful schools and their weaker brethren, and that may not be good for college sports in the long run.

Cuban argues that the amount of television money each school gets would drop and that scheduling will get worse. It's hard to determine if that will actually happen, though. The existing television contracts will certainly be drastically altered if superconference expansion goes ahead, and recent conference deals such as the Pac-12's suggest that not only could they be altered to higher numbers, but also that the potential is there for massive multi-network deals. The Pac-12 currently plans to work with both ESPN and FOX as well as launching six of their own regional networks; deals along those lines could solve issues along both the money and scheduling fronts.

Conference realignment is nothing new, of course; schools have been remaking conferences for decades. Each of those moves, like the demise of the old Southwestern Conference and the Big Eight, the Big East–ACC turf wars and the recent expansions of the Big 10 and the Pac-12, have had ripple effects, and none of them could have been completely predicted. If superconferences do come to pass, it seems likely the same thing will happen. Some effects, both positive and negative, can be anticipated at this point, but many are still yet to be seen. At this point, there's plenty for fans to be excited about—but also plenty to be wary of.

Student-Athletes, Schools, and Conferences Gain Power as the NCAA's Wanes

Andy Uhler

Andy Uhler is the Austin, Texas-based reporter for National Public Radio's (NPR) Marketplace. He joined the Marketplace team from the Texas Standard, *an hour-long news program produced at KUT in Austin, Texas.*

For a while now, the business of big-money college sports—mainly football and men's basketball—was pretty predictable and stable. The NCAA made the rules, conferences and schools cashed the checks and players got scholarships.

But that structure is unraveling.

Players have been winning the right to earn money in some ways. And in June, the Supreme Court struck a blow against the NCAA's ability to make rules when it unanimously decided that the organization is subject to antitrust law. Justice Brett Kavanaugh wrote that its business practices would be "flatly illegal in almost any other industry."

On the face of it, student athletes have been the big winners at this point in the challenge to college sports' status quo.

So far, 24 states have legislation on the books allowing players to make money off their names, images and likenesses, or NIL.

There's no national policy, but the NCAA has said it won't penalize any athlete, no matter what state they play in, who sells their NIL rights.

As a result, those athletes will be looking to go to schools that give them the most exposure.

"Student Athletes, Schools and Conferences Gain Power as NCAA's Wanes," by Andy Uhler, Minnesota Public Radio, August 13, 2021. Reprinted by permission.

And colleges are using their leverage to give the best athletes what they want, according to Patrick Rishe, director of the sports business program at Washington University in St. Louis.

"The major universities, because they are major universities in college athletics, they are going to have more eyeballs on them—whether it's Texas, Ohio State, or in basketball, Duke and Kentucky and North Carolina," he said. "So they do have a built-in advantage, so to speak."

Just a few weeks ago, two of those schools made a move to increase their advantage.

The University of Texas—the biggest moneymaker in college football, according to the *Wall Street Journal*—along with its bitter rival, Oklahoma University—ranked No. 7—announced that they will be leaving their longtime conference, the Big 12, to join the Southeastern Conference. That conference just signed a $300 million TV deal with ESPN that will allow the SEC to pay its member schools almost twice what the Big 12 paid its members last year.

"I think if you are an institution like Oklahoma and Texas that have the kind of brand equity in college football that they have, they're both in a position to be able to examine these options and essentially choose from the things they might want to do," said Michael Butterworth, director of the Center for Sports Communication & Media at the University of Texas at Austin.

But it's not just your Texases and Oklahomas that are trying to cash in. Just last year, more than 10 schools transferred their entire sports programs to new conferences. That included the 13,000-student Stephen F. Austin State University in Nacogdoches, Texas, which on July 1 moved from the Southland Conference to the Western Athletic Conference.

"We're trying to predict the future," said Ryan Ivey, the athletic director at Stephen F. Austin. "If we choose to make this move, is it going to achieve the goals that we set out to achieve?"

Ivey said his school's goals include increasing awareness in some bigger cities and possibly getting more money.

"Obviously, the opportunity that we felt from a revenue standpoint was there, whether that's the traditional TV contracts or whether that's the additional ticket sales, you know, donations, those types of things that were going to excite our fan base," he said.

Ivey said changing conferences cost Stephen F. Austin about $300,000. Texas and Oklahoma could pay more than $100 million combined to move to the SEC.

But Ellen Zavian, sports law professor at George Washington University, said these moves are long plays. Ultimately, she wouldn't be surprised to see the largest conferences go out on their own.

"Walk away from the NCAA, create their own entity, get their own deals done in all aspects and really negotiate with other conferences, a championship," she said.

But that sort of complete realignment would come with its own set of issues, according to Matt Mitten at the National Sports Law Institute at Marquette University.

"How do they reallocate rule- and decision-making power? How will the schools choose to do that, essentially, among themselves?" Mitten asked.

Because colleges don't want to have to pay athletes out of their budgets even as TV contracts continue to climb into the stratosphere.

Superconferences Will Benefit Major Programs

Mark Anderson

Mark Anderson has worked at the Las Vegas Review-Journal *since January 1999. He covered UNLV football for 17 seasons before moving to the men's basketball beat in January 2016. He was president of the Football Writers Association of America in 2016.*

When COVID-19 nearly wrecked the 2020 college football season, UNLV's scheduled trip to Iowa State was moved back a decade.

Having already been moved once, the game could be completely wiped out by 2030, not because of a global pandemic but by a desire by the Power Five conferences for even more control, power and money.

Those football conferences, plus Notre Dame, could be in a completely separate division well before then, forcing UNLV and other programs outside the Power Five to compete on their own and without the ability to play big-money games on big-time stages.

With the ability of college athletes to make money from their name, image and likeness already the law in several states and with a Supreme Court case that asks whether the NCAA's restrictions on compensation for student-athletes are in violation of federal antitrust law, the gap between the haves and have-nots in the college football world is about to widen.

Given their larger fan bases and wider media exposure, football players at Power Five conferences would be much better positioned to cash in on the new NIL regulations, giving those programs an even greater advantage in recruiting than they already enjoy.

"Seismic Change Coming Soon to Major College Football," by Mark Anderson, *Las Vegas Review-Journal*, June 11, 2021. Reprinted by permission.

UNLV athletic director Desiree Reed-Francois said through a spokesman that she wanted to withhold comment for now on a potential Power Five football breakaway, but that the school was working on an NIL plan.

On Thursday, the College Football Playoff management committee proposed expanding the playoff field from four to 12 teams, with six spots reserved for the highest-ranked conference champions and the other six going to at-large selections.

Such a field could include the Mountain West champion, giving UNLV a potential path into the playoffs. MW Commissioner Craig Thompson is on that committee.

But should the ACC, SEC, Big Ten, Pac-12 and Big-12 break away, they could create their own postseason format that doesn't include those other programs.

A Long Time Coming

The Power Five conferences have been consolidating control for many years in preparation for such a move.

"College football has clearly broken away anyway," University of Southern California sports business expert David Carter said. "The autonomy five or whatever they want to be called these days, they are running it more so than the NCAA."

To that end, the Knight Commission, the organization that carries great influence with college athletic administrators, has proposed a formal removing of all the top-tier, NCAA Division I football programs, the FBS to which UNLV belongs, from under the NCAA umbrella.

The commission issued a report in December called "Transforming the NCAA D-I model" that creates a separate governance structure for FBS programs that would be called the National College Football Association.

"FBS football generates the largest amount of revenue as it relates to all of college sports, and yet there's not single entity in control of and responsible for the sport," Knight Commission

CEO Amy Privette Perko said. "So the governance of the sport is fragmented between the College Football Playoff, the conferences and then the role that the NCAA does play."

That role, Perko pointed out, includes assuming the legal responsibility for the sport and overseeing the regular season, all done without receiving any revenue.

Economics, several experts said, would be the driving force behind any kind of FBS or Power Five football breakaway, whether it's formal or informal.

ESPN college basketball analyst Jay Bilas, a former Duke basketball player and outspoken critic of the NCAA, said the power conferences already are moving to a point where they play only each other in football and men's basketball.

"The days of being able to schedule a game and everybody's just going to go, those days are over," Bilas said. "Expectations are higher now, and there's more competition for spectators' time and attention. The students don't go as often as they used to. They want to go to the bigger games, so they're not as interested in seeing these other games."

NIL Legislation Impact

Athletes' ability to profit off their name, image and likeness is the next likely flash point that will determine the future state of the NCAA.

It's an issue the NCAA has fought for many years, maintaining such payments are counter to the contention that its athletes are amateurs. But on this issue, momentum is against the organization.

Many states have passed or are considering passing legislation to allow athletes to benefit from NIL. Those state decisions caused the NCAA to put together a working group last year to craft a proposal that is expected to be voted on June 22 or 23 by the Division 1 Council.

Regardless of what the NCAA does, laws take effect July 1 in Alabama, Florida, Georgia, Mississippi and New Mexico that allow athletes to accept endorsement deals. The same is true in Arizona beginning July 23.

Laws in 12 more states will be enacted next year and beyond, including Nevada in 2022. Assembly Bill 254 takes effect Jan. 1, and it was passed overwhelmingly 34-8 in the Assembly and unanimously in the Senate. Gov. Steve Sisolak signed the bill on May 29.

Congress also is considering passing legislation to establish uniform national standards.

Bilas said that while the NCAA has repeatedly fought the athletes' ability to make money off their NIL, they have been silent when it comes to coaches and athletic departments enriching themselves.

Money, he said, was the reason those departments continued to play games even during the height of the COVID-19 pandemic.

"We played because the institutions owed content to media-rights companies, and in order to get paid for that content, they had to play and provide the content," Bilas said. "That's demonstrable by a single question. Name me one nonathlete that the university put on an airplane for a university function last year. There's not one. So other students wanted to participate in their chosen field of endeavor, but they weren't allowed to."

Supreme Court to Weigh In

Right around the time the NCAA makes a decision on NIL, the U.S. Supreme Court will announce its determination on *NCAA v. Alston*. At stake is whether the NCAA remains exempt from antitrust laws to maintain current amateurism rules.

A federal district judge last year ruled the NCAA could not limit athletes' educational benefits, such as receiving equipment such as laptops or monetary grants for academic accomplishments. The NCAA argued that allowing athletes to receive such benefits would create a loophole that could be exploited to provide recruiting enticements that would more closely resemble pay for play.

The NCAA's stance didn't seem to fly with the Supreme Court justices during oral arguments on March 31. The newest member, Amy Coney Barrett, asked why the NCAA gets to decide how athletes earn money. Justice Samuel Alito noted athletes already receive compensation in the form of scholarships and stipends.

"The bottom line is that leaders understand the status quo is going to change," Perko said. "There will be major changes in college sport, so I think most leaders want to better understand how this new structure might address some of the questions around antitrust challenges for the future and how this model will make it better for universities, better for athletes."

No one knows for sure how the Power Five football programs would create their own division, other than it likely will occur sooner rather than later given the NIL and Supreme Court decisions that are coming.

Also worth watching is what happens with the TV contracts. Over a three-year period beginning in 2023, contracts will up for renewal for four of the Power Five conferences and the College Football Playoff. The Atlantic Coast Conference signed a 20-year contract with ESPN in 2016.

The Power Fives could spend the time before those deals expire positioning themselves for even grander paydays.

A Potential Blueprint

If the Knight Commission gets its way, there will be central leadership for all 10 FBS conferences. Perko pointed out the last major change to college athletics' structure occurred in 1973 when the three divisions were formed.

"The commission believes it's time for another evolution structure," she said. The evolution could play out even more dramatically.

The Power Fives could form a clean break, and the Knight Commission's governance model would apply to those schools. Maybe the Power Fives take the best of the best and create their own Super League.

"Just because you're in the Big Ten doesn't mean you automatically get a spot," Carter said of such a scenario. "How is Purdue going to feel? How will Mississippi State or Oregon State feel if they don't make it? Are they going to litigate?

"Think about it from a booster standpoint, a different piece of that. If my school didn't get it, yeah I'm angry, but if I'm on the outside looking in, what's the point in donating to Oregon State at this point if they're going to be playing in some other conference alignment or some other structure?"

It's a question that could be asked at programs, including UNLV, throughout the nation.

Athletes Should Flee the Socialist NCAA for Capitalist Pro Sports Organizations

Harrison Burge

Harrison Burge is a business and data analyst.

The college bowl season is in full swing. Some call it the most wonderful week of the year.

LSU, Stanford, and Baylor are among the teams playing this week. But for LSU running back Leonard Fournette, Stanford running back Christian McCaffrey, and Baylor running back Shock Linwood, their collegiate careers are over. When their teams take the field, instead of their usual view from the backfield, Fournette, McCaffrey, and Linwood will be watching from the sidelines.

Each has chosen to voluntarily skip his respective bowl game.

As NFL-bound prospects with potential millions to lose if seriously injured before draft day 2017, economic calculation came barreling in like the defensive lineman, linebackers, and secondary that this trio faced each Saturday.

These players chose tangible NFL future earnings—indeed life-altering money—over any of the intangibles associated with collegiate athletics: enjoyment of a final game with teammates, the opportunity to represent their universities one last time, or the possibility of a decisive performance in a victory to advance their namesake with their alma mater.

Central Planners at the NCAA

Over the past week-plus, these decisions to sit over play have echoed across both the college and professional football landscapes, attracting supporters, detractors, and a whole lot of controversy.

But, more importantly and not as well-reported or maybe even understood, these decisions have revealed the socialist disincentives of collegiate athletics versus the market incentives of private professional sports and how a player's subjective value navigates these two very different worlds.

Guided by a central planning committee known as the NCAA, this arbitrary-rule making authority attempts to override basic tenets of human action, and in so doing creates mass disincentives for student athletes in collegiate athletics.

The NCAA's rules ask us to imagine that any given college team is not made up of individuals with varying aptitudes, skills, and productivity. For instance, from a college team's lowliest player on athletic scholarship to the team's star (assuredly on scholarship as well), there is no market-coordinating system to reward high achievement.

A scholarship that covers tuition, room, and board plus a small stipend may be commensurate compensation for the athlete with the lowest marginal productivity. But for the team's star, whose efforts may single-handedly lead to higher ticket and merchandising sales for the university, he or she receives the exact same compensation for high marginal productivity.

Pay Everyone but Athletes?

Hamstrung by no less than the NCAA commissar's decree, the team's star will share in exactly zero percent of this increased revenue that he or she is directly responsible for. In an era of skyrocketing salaries for athletic directors, coaches, and professional athletes, how patient will the professional-bound college athlete be to remain an amateur?

How long will they tolerate going without present compensation and increased fulfillment of present needs and wants from the money they could have obtained? In other words, how strong is their time preference for the present versus the future?

An athlete's subjective value answers these questions. In his treatise, *Man, Economy, and State*, the great economist Murray Rothbard wrote, "the individual's value scale provides the key to the determination of all events on the market."

Indeed. And in economics, it matters not what individuals think. It matters what they do that displays their value scale in action.

In skipping their bowl games, Fournette, McCaffrey, and Linwood have displayed that their value scales rank future earnings over a final collegiate game and risk of injury that may impair these future earnings. While only time will tell if skipping bowl games will be a new trend for NFL-bound athletes, trends over the last decade show that underclassmen—individuals skipping an entire year of college eligibility—declaring for the NFL draft has more than doubled over this time period.

Capitalist Sports Beats Socialist Sports

Despite the path to stardom and riches in professional sports hardly guaranteed, the number of athletes who forego present satisfactions to pursue what they perceive is even greater opportunity in the future is indicative of incentives colliding with human action.

If university revenues increase courtesy of athletics while high-caliber athletes remain mired in a socialist collective existence, devoid of the opportunity for a market-based compensation, high-performing college athletes may increasingly look to the market of professional sports sooner.

Better Budgeting Can Prevent Revenue Loss for Athletic Programs

David Ridpath

David Ridpath is associate professor and Kahandas Nandola Professor of Sports Administration at Ohio University. As an expert in intercollegiate athletics administration, governance, rules, and compliance, he examines issues including student athlete academic achievement, academic fraud, and graduation rates.

The coronavirus continues to jeopardize college sports.

The NCAA men's and women's basketball tournaments were canceled back in the spring. In early August, smaller conferences like the Mid-American Conference and the Mountain West Conference postponed all fall sports, including football.

But the big news came when the Big 10 and PAC 12 postponed all fall 2020 sports until the spring. These comprise two of the Power Five conferences, which control the college football playoffs and earn the lion's share of revenue from the sport. The other Power Five conferences—the SEC, ACC and Big 12—are holding out hope that they can still play football in the fall.

The schools weighing whether to postpone are taking into account the health of staff and student athletes. But top of mind has to also be the financial implications of canceling a season, with Power Five conference schools facing the biggest repercussions.

Football: A Financial Pillar

Since many Power Five athletic programs are funded by football and basketball revenue, not having a football season would be a huge financial setback.

According to Patrick Rishe, director of the Sports Business Program at Washington University in St. Louis, each Power Five school would see an average loss of at least US$62 million in football revenue. This money is primarily generated from existing television contracts and sponsorships, in addition to football ticket sales. So even a season with empty or partially filled stadiums can earn a school a big paycheck.

On average, Power Five athletic departments—many with $100 million-plus budgets—make nearly half of their total operating revenue from football, with some schools deriving over 80% of department revenue from the sport. Typically this revenue funds the bulk of department operations including other sports programs and, in rare cases, even provides additional revenue to the academic side of the university.

The amount of money at stake explains why some Power Five conferences are desperately trying to figure out a way to make the season work. Before the PAC 12 and Big 10 bowed out, all the schools had altered their football schedules so that they would primarily play only conference games, similar to the amended Major League Baseball schedule. The idea was to reduce travel—and potential exposure to COVID-19—while still being able to have a season.

Not All Funding Models Are the Same

Where does the elimination of non-conference games among Power Five schools leave smaller schools? Is there a financial ripple effect?

Every year, mid-major programs—like those in the Group of Five conferences—play what are called "money games." In exchange for a large paycheck that sometimes exceeds $1 million, these schools will play a game against a Power Five school. Although there's the occasional upset of a Power Five team by a smaller school, these games are usually lopsided and only serve the purpose of earning extra money for the smaller school.

When several Group of Five conferences postponed fall sports, some in the media wondered whether it was motivated by finances, arguing that the schools couldn't afford to play a season without these guaranteed, non-conference money games.

While this money can certainly buttress an athletic department's budget, it doesn't mean that without them, a Group of Five program would cease to exist. Overall revenue from these games rarely exceeds 5% of the overall athletic budget of any Group of Five school. So the budget impact of money games is overstated.

We can see this in a database provided by The Knight Commission on Intercollegiate Athletics that breaks down the college athletic budgets at all NCAA Division I schools. Most Group of Five conference schools are subsidized somewhere between 60% and 90% from institutional support and student fees.

Using the Mid-American Conference as an example, the database shows for all schools in the conference that football games only represent 5% of overall athletic revenue. In the 2018-2019 season, no school derived more than 8% of its yearly take from these games, while for one school, The University of Toledo, it only amounted to 2%.

In other words, these departments don't need football to compete financially. While revenue loss can hurt, better budgeting can mitigate any shortfall.

So for many big conference schools, the cancellation of a football season can decimate an athletic department's budget, dragging down other sports in its wake. But for smaller conferences, student fees, not football, foot the bill—with enrollment drops presenting the real financial threat to athletic budgets.

Chapter 4

Is the Name, Image, and Likeness Rule Reasonable?

Overview: New Name, Image, and Likeness Rules Are Changing College Sports

Paul Sarker

Paul Sarker is an attorney who represents clients ranging from established industry leaders to emerging players across a wide spectrum of practice areas within entertainment, sports, and media.

On June 30, 2021, The National Collegiate Athletic Association (NCAA) Board of Directors approved a dramatic, albeit interim, revision to the NCAA's long-standing policy against student-athletes earning compensation. Effective July 1, 2021, student-athletes may receive compensation for the use of their name, image, and likeness (NIL), subject to compliance with applicable state law and other requirements (e.g., schools cannot compensate student-athletes for performance or recruitment—so-called "pay-for-play"). While this revision is being presented as "temporary," it may have been the NCAA's only viable remaining option while it waits for Congress to establish a nationwide NIL framework. Although significant details remain uncertain, the potential impacts on college athletics are game-changing.

This departure from the NCAA's prior position regarding "amateurism" was issued in response to (i) the June 21, 2021, 9-0 Supreme Court ruling in *NCAA vs. Alston et al.* (594 U.S. __,) which essentially held that the NCAA's rules limiting the education-related benefits that schools may make available to student-athletes are anti-competitive horizontal restraints of trade; and (ii) the enactment of NIL laws in several states (e.g., Alabama, Florida, Georgia, Mississippi, New Mexico, and Ohio) that are scheduled to go into effect July 1, 2021, and that are in direct conflict with the NCAA's previous policy. In addition

"Game-Changer: NCAA Revises Rules Governing Student-Athletes' Name, Image, and Likeness Rights," by Paul Sarker, The National Law Review, July 1, 2021. Reprinted by permission.

to these states, as many as 15 others have enacted or are in the process of enacting NIL legislation. Differences among states with respect to NIL may materially impact recruiting and a student-athlete's choice of college.

In an attempt to strike a balance between the NCAA's desire to preserve amateurism and the realities of the modern marketplace (i.e., (i) that college athletics is big business and (ii) that athletes are also potential influencers who should be able to monetize their brand without fear of compromising their eligibility), the NCAA has approved policy changes that pave the way for student-athletes to earn compensation while maintaining their amateur status. Previously, the NCAA permitted student-athletes to receive only limited consideration from their schools in the form of scholarships, meals, and reasonable expense allowances for travel, equipment, and health care, but until this revision, student-athletes were not allowed to receive consideration, meals, travel, or other items of value from third parties, agents, and/or representatives. While the extent of the consideration remains to be seen, there are opportunities for student-athletes to earn significant amounts for autographs, endorsements, personal appearances, paid social media, etc.

Framework

During their June 30, 2021, meeting, the NCAA Board of Governors adopted the following rudimentary framework:

1. Student-athletes will be able to earn compensation from the use of their NIL rights, provided that if such student-athlete is in a state that has enacted NIL legislation, the arrangement must comply with applicable state law.
2. Schools and conferences may not compensate student-athletes for performance ("pay-for-play" is still prohibited).

3. Student-athletes may engage the services of a professional (e.g., lawyer, agent, etc.) to assist in the monetization of their NIL.
4. Schools (and conferences) are tasked with determining whether the compensation complies with applicable state law and/or other applicable school or conference requirements.
5. Students-athletes will have to report their NIL compensation to their respective schools and conferences.

Open Questions

While this development may well lead to a surge in NIL deals for student-athletes, open questions remain, including:

1. What forms of consideration are permissible, apart from monetary consideration (cash)? In-kind consideration (e.g., a vehicle for tweeting about a car dealership) or other forms of consideration (e.g., equity in a joint venture, cryptocurrency)?
2. How will the member schools and conferences distinguish between acceptable endorsement deals and impermissible "pay-for-play" arrangements? Will there be a review board, or audit rights, or certification requirements?
3. What will the actual reporting requirements be? Will there be limits or other caps on the consideration that may be earned? How will these rules be enforced (e.g., loss of scholarship, fines, vacating wins)?
4. How will schools and conferences located in states that have not enacted NIL laws adapt? Will they default to the most permissive requirements in order to entice student-athletes?

5. How will this impact recruiting? Given the uncertainty and desire to maintain a competitive balance, will the federal government establish a national regime?

The immense appeal of sports, the broad reach of television and social media, and the rise of influencer culture and blockchain monetization (e.g., NFTs) are all factors that contribute to the enormous potential for student-athletes to monetize their NIL rights.

This potential coupled with the evolving legal and business landscape, the current state-by-state approach, and the significant open questions listed above regarding permissibility, reporting, and enforcement make it critical for student-athletes to be well-informed as they license their NIL rights. Further, companies looking to license student-athletes' NIL rights will, by and large, be sophisticated.

Given these factors, a knowledgeable advisor can be an invaluable resource to help parties: research, clarify, and comply with applicable legal requirements; understand the marketplace and their relative value within it; negotiate, structure, and draft NIL deals to maximize and protect that value; evaluate the various forms of consideration and risks presented by these deals; and assist in the enforcement of the deals once they have been papered, including with litigation, if necessary.

The Name, Image, and Likeness Law Will Bring New Opportunities to College Athletes

Edgardo J. Mantilla

Edgardo J. Mantilla is a patent attorney at Caldwell Intellectual Property Law.

Many professional athletes know the benefits of using their name, image, and likeness ("NIL") for commercial purposes. For many, this serves as a lucrative enterprise outside their actual sporting arena where athletes, for instance, may use their image to promote/endorse a product.[1] However, profiting from one's NIL has been forbidden by rules applicable to college athletes as a form of financial compensation for athletic activity. Recently, a lot has been publicized about the upcoming changes to the National Collegiate Athletic Association ("NCAA") bylaws surrounding NIL. In general, NIL are three elements related to the legal concept of right of publicity, a doctrine dating to the 19th century when it was introduced in a *Harvard Law Review* article written by Louis Brandeis and Samuel Warren.[2] The right of publicity allows anyone to commercialize their NIL and/or prevent unauthorized use for commercial purposes of their NIL.

Common examples of NIL in the professional sports space include the usage of an athlete's name on a jersey for sale, an athlete making an appearance on a commercial or advertisement, and a computer-generated image of an athlete appearing in a video game. However, unlike their professional counterparts, college athletes have never had an opportunity to earn money from their name, image, and likeness. However, as of July 1st 2021, depending on states' NIL laws, all NCAA athletes are

"Name, Image, Likeness, and Interplay with Intellectual Property," Edgardo J. Mantilla, Patent Attorney, Caldwell Intellectual Property Law, JD Supra, LLC, July 8, 2021. Reprinted by permission.

allowed to make money from a wide variety of business ventures without losing their eligibility.

This post will discuss what potential considerations would need to be addressed regarding intellectual property, more specifically trademarks, as athletes venture to market their NIL to generate revenue.

Legal and Legislative History Involving the NCAA and NIL

There is no federal statue directly governing NIL, and so its history has been driven by state laws and federal court decisions sounding in antitrust law. For instance, in the 1984 opinion in *National Collegiate Athletic Ass'n v. Board of Regents of the University of Oklahoma*, the Supreme Court struck down a proposed television plan proposed by the NCAA as anticompetitive, but in doing so, it also gave the NCAA latitude to maintain "a revered tradition of amateurism in college sports."[3] The NCAA has maintained that antitrust law permits them to eliminate any sort of athlete compensation to promote competitive equity and to distinguish college athletics from professional sports.

In 2009, Ed O'Bannon, a former UCLA men's basketball player, filed a lawsuit against the NCAA and the Collegiate Licensing Company for the use of his likeness in the popular EA Sports video game *NCAA Basketball 09*. In 2014, the District Court ruled in favor of O'Bannon, which led to the discontinuation of the college sports-themed EA video games, intensifying the conversation regarding the compensation of student-athletes for use of their NIL.[4]

More recently, in June 2021, the Supreme Court issued an opinion in *National Collegiate Athletic Association. v. Alston*.[5] Current and former student-athletes brought this antitrust lawsuit challenging the NCAA's restrictions on compensation. The Court's unanimous decision, written by Justice Neil Gorsuch, upheld a district court order enjoined the NCAA from enforcing limits placed on education-related benefits, which include certain types of academic scholarships and related educational benefits provided by member schools to student athletes. Under the "Rule of Reason"[6] approach, the Court determined that the NCAA rules regarding limitations on educational benefits had an anticompetitive effect.[7] The Court noted that the student-athletes showed that the NCAA could maintain a distinction between college and professional sports (the "tradition of amateurism" referred in *Board of Regents of the University of Oklahoma* case) with substantially less restrictive alternative rules related to educational benefits.[8] The strongest statement against any compensation questions by the NCAA came on Justice Kavanaugh's concurrence, which stated that "the NCAA's current compensation regime raises serious questions under antitrust laws."[9] Moreover, any future antitrust question regarding compensation of athletes should be resolved using the "Rule of Reason" standard as opposed to any more lenient standard.[10]

The Supreme Court opinion in the *Alston* case and Justice Kavanaugh's concurrent opinion are at the center of current litigation related to NIL. In *Johnson v. NCAA*, a case in Pennsylvania federal court centering on whether college athletes are owed minimum wage protections, the presiding judge, John Padova, has asked the players and NCAA to file briefs explaining to what extent, the *Alston* ruling impacts their case.[11]

In another high-profile case, Oregon basketball player Sedona Prince has sued the NCAA seeking class certification in a case where she maintains denial of NIL violated antitrust laws, potentially leading to many millions of dollars in damages to athletes.[12] It is worth noting that the Prince's case is before Judge Wilken, who not only handled *Alston* but also presided over Ed O'Bannon's successful case against the NCAA.[13]

Besides the judiciary, state legislatures are enacting laws to enable athletes to receive compensation for their NIL. In September 2019, California became the first state to pass legislation to create a legal right for college athletes to be compensated for the commercial use of their identities. The "Fair Pay to Play" Act, which becomes effective in 2023, guarantees college athletes a right to profit from their identities. The Act also authorizes college athletes to hire agents and other representatives to assist them in negotiating and securing commercial opportunities.[14] This July 1st, laws allowing college athletes to earn money from use of their NIL became effective in some states such as Alabama, Colorado, Florida, Georgia, Illinois, Louisiana, Mississippi, New Mexico, Ohio, Oregon, Pennsylvania, and Texas.[15] Other states have taken the initiative as well and passed similar laws which are set to take effect within the next four years.[16]

NCAA Changes to NIL

On June 30, 2021, the governance bodies for NCAA Division I, II, and III sports adopted a uniform interim policy suspending NCAA name, image and likeness rules for all incoming and current student-athletes in all sports.[17] The interim policy includes guidelines, such as [18]

- Individuals can engage in NIL activities that are consistent with the law of the state where the school is located. Colleges and universities may be a resource for state law questions.
- College athletes who attend a school in a state without an NIL law can engage in this type of activity without violating NCAA rules related to name, image and likeness.
- Individuals can use a professional services provider for NIL activities.
- Student-athletes should report NIL activities consistent with state law or school and conference requirements to their school.

As mentioned before, currently state law applies to NIL statutes that could lead to confusion for student-athletes as different rules may apply in different states. The NCAA has engaged the United States Congress to persuade Congress into enacting a federal NIL statute.

Intellectual Property and NIL

For many college athletes, this area of commercializing their NIL is new to them. Because of the volume of athletes that will take advantage of changes to NIL by the NCAA, commercialization of NIL will become a very competitive space for the athletes. Athletes will be now eligible to monetize their social media accounts, sign autographs, coach camps, and participate in advertising campaigns. As such, athletes should protect their brands through an effective trademark strategy. There are multiple aspects of an athlete's NIL that can receive the benefits of trademark protection; these include, but are not limited to, the athlete's name, logo, or slogan.

The athlete's name is likely the first thing anyone will recognize and potentially associate with a product or brand, and most likely, the most important one in terms of requiring protection. A sound trademark strategy surrounding the athlete's name would not only allow a student athlete to control how their name is used commercially, but also, it may be used to deter and to defend against unauthorized use of the name. It is important to note that, since a trademark needs to be used in commerce, applying for a trademark just with a defensive intent is not good enough.[19]

Protecting a logo or a slogan gives the student-athlete the exclusive right to use, produce, copy, and profit from it. Something an athlete may say which is fairly known to fans may be used potentially in a branding campaign for the athlete. In addition, a logo makes it possible to connect, for example, a particular athlete's logo to what a company does. For example, most people will connect [the TB12 logo] (Registration 5,284,247) to Tom Brady (former quarterback of the New England Patriots and currently playing for the Tampa Bay Buccaneers) and his "TB12" health-related business.

By applying for a trademark for a logo, the athlete decides where the logo appears, how the logo is updated or amended, and which parties may license it for use in their own materials.

Last Remarks…

The changes to NIL bylaws by the NCAA will bring many opportunities for student-athletes to commercialize their name, image, and likeness. However, this commercialization process can be complex and challenging. Filling the appropriate trademarks will provide the necessary protection for an effective and lucrative branding campaign. Besides agents and public relations specialist, student-athletes should engage a trademark attorney as part of their team, who can provide guidance regarding how to develop a trademark strategy to protect and commercialize their brand.

Notes

1. https://youtu.be/ITDFgsRIryg
2. Samuel D. Warren and Louis Brandeis, *The Right to Privacy*, 4 Harv. L. Rev. 193, 195 (1890) ("Recent inventions and business methods call attention to the next step which must be taken for the protection of the person, and for securing to the individual … the right 'to be let alone' …")
3. *National Collegiate Athletic Ass'n v. Board of Regents of the University of Oklahoma*, 468 U.S. 85, 120 (1984)
4. *O'Bannon v. NCAA*, 7 F. Supp. 3d 955, 962-63 (N.D. Cal. 2014)
5. *National Collegiate Athletic Association v. Alston*, 594 U.S. ___ (2021)
6. *Chicago Board of Trade v. United States*, 246 U.S. 231 (1918)
7. *National Collegiate Athletic Association*, 594 U.S. ___ at 22
8. *Id.* at 4
9. *Id.* at 42 (Kavanaugh, J., concurring)
10. *Id.* ("After today's decision, the NCAA's remaining compensation rules should receive ordinary 'rule of reason' scrutiny under the antitrust laws")
11. https://www.sportico.com/law/analysis/2021/supreme-court-ruling-alston-1234632592/
12. *Id*
13. *Id*

14. Collegiate athletics: student athlete compensation and representation Cal. S. SB-206 (2019-2020), Chapter 383 (Cal. Stat. 2019).

15. https://theathletic.com/2580642/2021/07/01/name-image-and-likeness-nil-what-it-means-why-it-matters-and-how-it-will-impact-college-sports/

16. *Id*

17. https://www.ncaa.org/about/resources/media-center/news/ncaa-adopts-interim-name-image-and-likeness-policy

18. *Id*

19. 15 U.S.C § 1527

Student-Athletes Should Be Paid

College Sports Madness

College Sports Madness is a website that specializes in paying attention to and writing about all college sports, covering small college sports in addition to major programs.

College sports brings a lot of money to advertisers and college administrations, but the only people who don't get any financial benefit are the student athletes themselves. The public does not know that a college athlete doesn't receive any compensation for his efforts, even if he sacrifices a lot to achieve success in the chosen sport. In this essay, we will explore the reasons why paying college athletes is a fair thing to do and give you examples of similar mistreatment.

Whether college athletes should be paid is a topic of debate among students, college managers, and the private companies that want students to promote their brands and products in the field. Are you looking to learn more about this? Why do student athletes deserve a share of the game profits?

1. Sports Take as Much Time as a Full-Time Job

Various statistics suggest that college athletes spend at least 40 hours per week dedicated to their sport, including games and training sessions. This is like working a full-time job on top of demanding courses, school assignments, and other responsibilities. Without putting intense working hours, a student athlete cannot remain on the team or keep his scholarship. For all the time they put into ensuring the success of their team, students deserve to be paid for their efforts.

"Top 10 Reasons College Athletes Should Be Paid," College Sports Madness, February 13, 2020. Reprinted by permission.

2. A Greater Stake for Students Will Make Games More Competitive

If they could hope for financial compensation, students will feel motivated to raise their level of performance. Good earnings will increase students' motivation to work harder to rise and maintain their ranking. In addition, students will feel less stressed about their financial situation so they can focus more on the games without money anxiety.

3. Athletes Take Time Away from Study to Play Sports

To do great things with his team, a college athlete must make sport his first priority, which leads him to put fewer hours into studying than a non-athlete. This impacts his academic performance with long-term effects in his future professional career. As we can see in this research paper on should college athletes be paid, success in sports comes sometimes to the detriment of academic achievement. Read essay examples to educate yourself as to why paying athletes is necessary in this case.

4. Coaches Receive Extravagant Salaries

While the importance of good coaches cannot be underestimated, coaches of high-achieving teams receive extravagant salaries considering that they share their workload with several assistants. In addition, as employees of an academic institution, coaches receive salaries that are unfair compared to what teachers and professors with advanced degrees earn, according to essay samples on the topic. Some coaches receive millions of dollars a year and student athletes receive nothing, even if there's plenty of money going around.

5. College Sports Money Is Not Used for Students' Benefit

The huge revenues in college athletics are not going to research or education investments, so the students sometimes see no return on their efforts to maintain their team in the rankings. Instead of going to students and university facilities, the earnings are split between coaches and administrations in the form of huge salaries. In fact, some colleges are forced to use their budgets to fund the athletic departments.

6. College Athletes Must Pay for Expenses from Their Pockets

Many student athletes are on full scholarships, so their tuition, college fees, and accommodation are covered by their institution. However, there are other expenses involved in being an athlete that students must cover with their personal money. Examples of crucial expenses are food or wardrobe for special events. Maybe they need to pay for an essay online to be able to attend a game. Since some students come from modest backgrounds, there's no one to cover for these expenses and their parents cannot support them.

7. Sports Teams Increase the Status of Their Colleges

The achievements of the student athletes translate into fame and higher status for their colleges. This means the college gets the chance to attract more academic and sports talent and to increase its tuition fees according to its popularity. Through their success, college athletes give their colleges the opportunity to be more selective in the admission process and get more recognition.

8. A Salary Would Help Student Athletes Invest in Their Future

By having a salary, college athletes would leave school not just with a degree, but with significant savings as well, which will help them begin their adult life securely. In addition, not all student athletes get drafted in a salaried position on a sports team when they graduate. This puts them in a tough spot once they're out of college. If they don't end up playing professional sports, all their efforts leave them with nothing.

9. College Is a Highly Profitable Industry

College athletics is an industry of billions of dollars of revenue across all sports. Student athletes who play especially football, basketball or baseball bring in millions of dollars to their athletics department. These vast revenues are unfairly distributed considering that the main people who make this happen, the players, receive nothing.

10. Students Are Not Cheap Labor

In this current state of affairs, it seems that student athletes are nothing but cheap labor meant to fatten the accounts of executives, coaches and college administrations. All the excuses that managers have for not paying students are ridiculous and have been proven wrong. A thorough analysis suggests that students are simply discriminated against receiving part of the earnings they generate simply because they get a scholarship. However, the scholarship is hardly enough to compensate them for their efforts.

Playing sports in college comes at a great mental and physical cost for students, yet they get no word into how the big earnings should be distributed. There are plenty of reasons to believe that this situation should change.

The New NCAA Endorsement Rules Could Benefit Women More Than Men

Lindsey Darvin

Lindsey Darvin is assistant professor of sport management at State University of New York College at Cortland. She teaches courses on intercollegiate sport, sport ethics, and sport sociology. She received her Ph.D. from the University of Florida in health and human performance with a concentration in sport management.

Only one week after the NCAA changed its endorsement rules on July 1, 2021, women college athletes found themselves on billboards in Times Square in New York, launching a clothing line collaboration and signing sponsorship deals for brands including a wireless carrier and a fast-food chain.

Women college athletes have historically been far more limited in their ability to profit off their athletic skills compared to their male counterparts. As an assistant professor of sport management who researches gender equity in college athletics, I believe the new name, image and likeness rules will begin to level the playing field.

In fact, women college athletes may have the most to gain from the NCAA change.

Highly Underrepresented

Throughout collegiate and professional sports, women are underrepresented among players, coaches, administrators and front office employees.

At best, the proportions of women working in college and professional sports have remained relatively stagnant over

"The New NCAA Endorsement Rules Could Benefit Women More Than Men," by Lindsey Darvin, The Conversation, September 29, 2021. https://theconversation.com/new-ncaa-endorsement-rules-could-benefit-women-more-than-men-166003.

the past decade, with some high-profile gains at the men's professional league levels.

Men account for roughly 60% of all NCAA women's program head coaches and 98% of men's program head coaches. Furthermore, 76% of Division 1 NCAA athletic directors, the highest administrative role, are held by white men.

These imbalances have caused many women college athletes to second-guess their ability to make a career in college coaching.

Much Lower Salaries

The average player salary in the WNBA is US$130,000, and the minimum salary is $59,000. In comparison, the average NBA salary for the 2021-2022 season is $7.5 million, with a minimum salary of roughly $925,000. The NBA minor league basketball organization, the NBA G League, pays select players $125,000 per season.

Women's tennis provides some of the highest player salaries at an average of roughly $285,000 per season, but the salary totals for professional women athletes in other sports drop significantly from that starting point.

For professional women's soccer, the average is $35,000. Professional men's soccer players earn roughly $400,000 on average.

For professional fast-pitch softball, the number falls to a mere $6,000 per season. The average salary for Major League Baseball, meanwhile, was roughly $4.2 million for the 2019 season.

So, even when women athletes play professionally, they often do not earn enough for it to be their sole occupation.

Fewer Opportunities to Go Pro

Women college athletes also have fewer opportunities to play their sport at the professional level. That is to say, making a professional team is even more difficult for women college athletes than men.

For example, the WNBA is the toughest North American professional sports league to earn a roster spot within, given the total number of teams and roster limits. The WNBA has only 12 teams, and each roster is limited to 12 players. For comparison, the NBA has 30 teams and the roster permits 15 total players, as well as 29 G League teams with no roster limit of up to 13 players.

Highly Marketable

Despite their limited sport career prospects, women college athletes are highly marketable. This is evident in the growth in viewership for events such as the NCAA women's gymnastics championship and the NCAA Women's College World Series. For the 2020 Women's College World Series, the average per game viewership was roughly 1.2 million, 10% higher than 2019. The 2020 women's gymnastics final averaged over 800,000 viewers—five times more viewers than in 2019.

Women college athletes have also been shown to be savvy social media users, with some gaining hundreds of thousands of followers.

In fact, one 2021 analysis of projected earnings conducted by the marketing platform Opendorse found that eight of the top 10 most followed social media profiles among NCAA Tournament Elite Eight basketball players belonged to women athletes. These numbers were calculated by combining their total number of Twitter and Instagram followers.

This equates to higher earning power, as the top two women's accounts range in potential endorsement value from $382,000 to $965,000 a year. Much of the earning potential is based on sponsored social media posts.

Some women college cheerleaders have already been earning upwards of $5,000 per Instagram post, as their sport is not governed by NCAA bylaws.

A similar 2020 analysis conducted by Athletic Director U found that, among all college athletes regardless of sport, more women than men—14 versus 11—are projected to be among the top 25 earners of endorsement revenue based on social reach. The annual projected endorsement potential for these top women college athletes ranged from $34,000 for Brooke Thomas of Oklahoma State University track and field to roughly $500,000 for Madison Kocian of UCLA gymnastics.

Some top women college athletes have been preparing for endorsement deals by signing contracts with talent management companies. Paige Bueckers, a University of Connecticut women's basketball player; Cameron Brink of Stanford women's basketball; and Sarah Fuller of Vanderbilt football and soccer are just a few of the college athletes that have recently signed with Wasserman, a sports marketing and talent management company based in Los Angeles.

These women college athletes now have a real opportunity to earn money off their skills as athletes in ways other professional sport career paths could never guarantee.

Hazards Loom as the NCAA Implements Name, Image, and Likeness

Andrew Perloff

Andrew Perloff is a freelance writer and producer and on-air contributor for the nationally syndicated sports radio show The Dan Patrick Show.

[…]

The NCAA has proven to be resilient in defending its amateur model in the past and could avoid paying players for years. But it will face challenges from multiple directions. Lawmakers who argued for NIL could push even further, demanding more direct compensation to players. An athlete could sue the NCAA or a conference and force the courts once again to expand player benefits. Or a group of players could lead the push.

Already, the organization seems on the losing end in the court of public opinion. In March 2021, Seton Hall University released its annual Sports Poll and reported that only 30 percent of respondents were against athletes in revenue-generating college sports being paid, compared to 60 percent in 2017 and 71 percent in 2013.

In an interview with reporters in July, NCAA president Mark Emmert suggested it was time to rethink the organization's role. "When you have an environment like that, it just forces us to think more about what constraints should be put in place ever on college athletes," he said. "And it should be the bare minimum."

This is a drastic change of direction for an organization that listed its legal fees at $68 million for the fiscal year 2019–20 to fight for its "core values." But admitting partial defeat may well be the organization's best hope for survival. By having a lighter touch, the NCAA can improve its chances of avoiding further antitrust litigation.

The new NIL rule has already provided opportunities for athletes to group together to gain leverage. It stands to reason that players organizing to establish wages might not be far off. In 2014, football players at Northwestern University attempted to form a union with the blessing of the Chicago office of the National Labor Relations Board. The university challenged the move, and the full National Labor Relations Board agreed. The local ruling was overturned, and the union was blocked because players were not considered employees.

But that was seven years ago. Another attempt by athletes might have different results in the current environment.

These trends bode well for players at bigger universities, especially in the South and Midwest where college football is as popular as the NFL. But what's good for athletes in revenue-generating sports like football and men's basketball might not work for everyone else. If the intercollegiate student-athlete model disappears, what else will disappear along with it? If the commercial upside to revenue-generating sports grows ever larger, will institutions be willing or able to pay for traditional money-losers that serve as feeders for U.S. Olympic teams, like diving, volleyball, and swimming?

During the pandemic, universities started cutting sports at an alarming rate to make up for lost revenue, with at least 350 programs eliminated nationwide in 2020 alone. Smaller school teams and less visible sports were most vulnerable and will continue to be endangered as revenue programs thrive. It may well be time for schools to consider the value of these programs, both in terms of helping meet federal requirements such as Title IX and supporting their institutional missions. But it also may be that these programs need to find more sustainable financial models. That could mean canceling programs or downgrading them from competitive divisions within NCAA sports to less formal club status.

It's also worth asking how allowing student-athletes to build and monetize their personal brands could affect colleges and classmates outside of the sports complex. After all, it is these athletes' classmates who help pay for college-sports programs through required annual fees buried within their tuition bills. In 2018, the 358 large colleges and universities classified as Division I schools collected $1.2 billion in student fees to support sports, up 51 percent from 10 years ago.

As Emmert said, this is the year to reconsider everything. Do big-time football programs fit alongside other college sports—which, at some schools, they partially subsidize—and should they continue to be held to the same rules? In considering alternatives, one approach would be for the most elite 65 schools, members of the "Power Five" conferences, to break off their football programs from the rest of the NCAA. There is already a precedent for this, such as post-season tournaments like the College Football Playoff. Or perhaps the football-heavy Southeastern Conference, which will grow to include powerhouse teams at the universities of Texas and Oklahoma by 2025, could take a more central role in leading the biggest programs.

The cultural impact of college sports runs deep. It is an important community builder for undergraduates. Games give students something to look forward to and rally around. At some places, especially in the South, college football is the one American sport that can rival international soccer for crowd engagement. If you get a chance to go to a night game at Louisiana State or sit in Kyle Field to watch the Texas A&M Aggies, you'll hear the loudest, most passionate fans in the nation.

But what does that look like on campus the next day? Can a football player generating a six-figure income still be considered a student? Will they be isolated from the rest of their student body?

The prospect of NIL endorsements has actually provided a surprising academic opportunity. Schools like the University of Nebraska, Florida State, Penn State, and the universities of Arkansas and Colorado were among the first to develop robust cross-departmental education programs to help student-athletes learn branding and marketing. Nebraska Athletics, which launched the #NILbraska program on its flagship campus in Lincoln in

June, stated its goal to create "a core curriculum that will benefit not just student-athletes, but all students on campus who may be interested in leveraging their personal brands." The entrepreneur-focused program was designed by business-school faculty and features pop-up classes across campus, including at the schools of communications and law.

We're about to see how NIL deals and performance on the field go together. This year's Chick-Fil-A kickoff game pits the Alabama Crimson Tide against the Miami Hurricanes, teams led by quarterbacks who are also leaders in signing NIL deals. In addition to King, Alabama's sophomore quarterback Bryce Young has reportedly signed more than $800,000 in NIL deals—sums that his coach called "ungodly." (His coach being Nick Saban, whose salary of $9.5 million this year makes him the highest-paid college coach in the nation.) Does this destroy the "joy" of the sport? Do we need our college stars to be humble and hungry? It's hard to imagine why that would be the case. Fans around the world are used to watching millionaires play games and are no less passionate about their favorite sports.

During oral arguments in *Alston*, Chief Justice John Roberts compared limiting the NCAA's powers to playing a precarious game of Jenga, in which players painstakingly remove blocks from a tower and lose if they cause it to fall. If we keep removing pieces of the NCAA's authority, will a once-solid base of college sports suddenly crumble? Or will the base for revenue-generating sports become even stronger? How will that affect other sports, other students, and entire campuses? This fast-moving period of change provides each school the opportunity to step back and decide which role it wants to play in the uniquely American phenomenon of college sports.

College Sports Still Exploit Athletes

Nathan Kalman-Lamb, Derek Silva, and Johanna Mellis

Nathan Kalman-Lamb, Derek Silva, and Johanna Mellis are co-hosts of The End of Sport *podcast.*

I think NIL is just to keep kids from going overseas, especially in basketball, to keep them in college. They're still not getting the cut they deserve. I think it's still a slave mentality."

That's how CJ Watson, a former University of Tennessee and NBA player, characterized the 1 July move by the NCAA, the main governing body of US college sport, to liberalize its policy on name, image, and likeness (NIL) rights. The decision permits college athletes to make money from things such as sponsorship and public appearances, activities that were once prohibited under the dubious rationale they would compromise the integrity of amateur sport (amateur sport, incidentally, in which the coaches and administrators often make millions of dollars a year).

For many proponents of reform in college sport, the news was heralded as a major victory. And, indeed, the denial of these rights was symptomatic of the exploitative economy of college athletics in the United States. Yet, to celebrate NIL rights—in some cases yielding as little as $3 per endorsement—as the end of racialized exploitation in college athletics obscures the reality highlighted by Watson: big-time college sport is often about rich white people using Black people for profit.

In his 2010 expose of the NCAA, sociologist Billy Hawkins traces the relationship between predominantly white colleges and universities (PWIs) and Black athletes. For Hawkins, the structure of big-time college sports reflect long-standing systems of economic, political, social, and cultural coercion, producing an "intercollegiate athletic industrial complex," at PWIs—a new version for a plantation mentality that has long exploited Black people in the US for economic gain.

NCAA sport was built upon the foundational racial inequalities of American society and higher education. White colonizers and later Americans established the first universities in the US on land stolen from Indigenous peoples, and built and paid for these institutions using the exploited labor of, and profits extracted from, enslaved people. American racial capitalism permeated the structure of higher education from the 1600s on. Though historically Black universities and colleges (HBCUs) served as the predominant places of university instruction and athletic success for Black people due to racial segregation, white-dominated state legislatures sought ways to reform and maintain their racial control over higher education when racial segregation was outlawed in the postwar era.

Generous state funding for PWIs and their athletic departments (in contrast to HBCUs) became an avenue to legally reshape the plantation system. Seeking to boost their athletic success and prestige, PWIs lured Black athletes away from HBCUs with scholarships and better facilities than HBCUs could offer. Hawkins shows how the racialized organizations of the NCAA created a system of internal colonization, where the dominant group of PWIs became the colonizers who "bought" Black athletes for their exploitative plantation system. The big colleges wielded the disciplinary cudgel of amateurism to prevent Black and Brown athletes from monetizing their labor through the specious goal of "protecting them from exploitation."

The plantation dynamics of college sport today are most readily apparent in the elite power five conferences (the ACC, SEC, Big Ten, Pac 12, and Big 12) and the sports that bring in the big money: football and basketball. In the 2018-2019 season, the 65 power five universities generated $8.3bn in revenue between them. Yes, 8.3 billion. As Watson succinctly puts it, "There's still a lot of revenue going out there." Yet, that money does not find its way into the pockets of the disproportionately Black athletes responsible for generating it. While only 5.7% of the students at the PWIs that make up the power five are Black, that number surges to 55.9% for men's basketball, 55.7% for football, and 48.1% for women's basketball. These athletes receive only cost of attendance scholarships in exchange for their labor. In many cases, they do not even receive health insurance.

So, where do those billions go? Well, the primary beneficiaries are the coaches, athletic department officials, and university presidents who oversee their work. White people disproportionately rule the campus athletic work in the power five conferences, whether at the level of chancellors and presidents (84%), athletic directors (75%), or head coaches (81% of men's basketball coaches, 82% of women's basketball coaches, and 80% of football coaches). The denial of compensation to the Black athletes who drive revenue is the single most damning dimension of the plantation dynamics of college sport.

Darius, a current SEC football player, told us: "It's frustrating for me because NIL doesn't change the fact that I show up every Saturday and play in front of thousands of screaming fans and everyone else gets paid."

David West, a former NBA all-star who now helps run the Professional Collegiate League, an alternative to NCAA competition, says: "Even with [NIL], the same mechanisms of control are still in place, meaning the system is still set up to benefit the players last, not first."

Connecticut senator Chris Murphy, co-sponsor of the pro-unionization College Athlete Right to Organize Act, agrees: "Majority-white executives have long exploited the talents and labor of majority Black college athletes, but America is finally waking up to the injustices that are inherent in college athletics. Giving athletes the ability to make money off their name, image, likeness should be considered the floor and not the ceiling. We must still ensure athletes receive fair compensation for their labor as well as health, safety and academic protections along with real power in their industry. This is a civil rights issue."

Grappling with the plantation dynamics of big-time college sport also requires confronting the insidious myth legitimizing them: that players consent to participate. What the insipid platitude that "they signed up for it" conveniently leaves out is the coercion at the heart of college athletics, even in the NIL era. This coercion comes in two forms.

First, the very decision to accept a scholarship and participate in big-time college sports is grounded in a form of racialized structural coercion. Borrowing from Jill Fisher, structural coercion refers to the social and economic conditions that shape the choices available to a person. The massive gap in social, economic, and cultural conditions produced by racial capitalism in US history, and the accompanying chasm in access to higher education and high-paying jobs, is exactly what structural coercion looks like. Today, Black families have less than 15% of the wealth of white families both on average and at the median. Moreover, while 45% of white 25-29 year olds have attained a bachelor's degree and 56% have attained an associate's degree, only 28% and 36% of Black Americans have. Given these disparities, a scholarship to participate in college sport becomes less a choice than a necessity.

Kaiya McCullough, a former UCLA and pro soccer player and co-founder of the United College Athlete Association says: "Educational compensation is a far cry from full compensation for the amount of labor done and revenue generated by college athletes, and any substantial change in plantation dynamics within college sport would have to address this issue."

Likewise, once on campus, athletes are confronted by a second form of coercion referred to by sociologist Erin Hatton as status coercion. Status coercion shows the myriad ways in which athletic departments exercise power over athletes by controlling chances to showcase their abilities in the hope of turning professional. The fact that coaches control whether an athlete plays means that they can also regulate what they are allowed to say and do via discipline and surveillance, fundamentally curtailing their freedom.

NIL rights do not resolve either structural or status coercion because college athletes must still remain in the good graces of their programs. For example if a football star isn't playing every week, he's unlikely to win a sponsorship from the local car dealer.

Ryan, a current Pac 12 player, says: "I don't think NIL has fundamentally changed the plantation dynamics of college sports. There isn't actually any pay for play. All that's guaranteed is some money that you can possibly make off your own name."

NIL also ushers a new era of gig-work into the lives of athletes—a labor environment literally subsidizing athletic departments by forcing players to seek out income from private companies. As Darius puts it: "It's like I'm a f****n' Uber driver delivering tacos except I'm out there hawking some BBQ joint for money I've already earned."

He continues, "no matter what they do, until we get paid for our work it's still going to be a bunch of white guys getting paid on the back of Black folk like me." Coaches and athletic department personnel reap the rewards of athletic labor whilst not paying the workers themselves. "In my eyes it's f*****," says Darius. "I gotta do even more work and everybody else is getting money that me and my brothers earn out there on the field." These are plantation dynamics, rearranged.

McCullough is also unsure about who benefits from NIL. "I think some of the same racial dynamics are replicated in [NIL]. Black athletes have the potential to generate large amounts of personal profit with their NIL, however, in most cases these athletes have little to no help on how to properly market themselves ... individuals with resources and access will be able to fully reap the benefits of NIL, while those who come from lower socioeconomic backgrounds with less professional connections may not."

Current WNBA player and WNBPA executive Elizabeth Williams sees NIL changes as "a step in the right direction," particularly for "women to profit in a way they could not in the past," but adds, "there are still certain players with access to resources like marketing and PR firms that Black players may not have access to."

There is another important dimension to the equation. According to the current logic of big-time college sport, universities pay their players in the form of a subsidized education. But, if education is compensation, any way in which that education is compromised amount to wage theft. This is particularly problematic for Black players at PWIs often made to feel they don't belong, including by professors. For Darius, "Some profs don't give a s*** about us, they see us as a nuisance or trouble or not worth their time … like we ain't even real students. I have had profs help me figure s*** out and really pay attention to my needs as someone who basically works a full time job for the university and I had profs who basically tell me I'm not a real student and I shouldn't be there."

The problem for racialized players, like all players, is, in part, the structural conditions of that education, which make learning almost impossible—athletes are commonly up before dawn, well before other students, for gym sessions and are often discouraged from taking classes that clash with training. Darius notes, "I want to further my education and all that, but sometimes that's hard when I can barely stay awake [because I'm] tired as f*** from practice. I don't even blame people for thinking I don't care about school … how can I after a three-hour practice, film session, and team meetings?"

So, has NIL revolutionized the plantation dynamics of college sport?

West says that "NIL hasn't fundamentally changed anything in college sports." For Darius, in the end, "This whole thing is built on sand and NIL won't change that." Ryan concludes: "Racial injustice is an ongoing issue that getting a cut of the revenue can help but not erase from revenue sport. NIL certainly doesn't do that." And for Watson, "They're still bringing in this fresh meat every year to build up the school's name and that's just going to continue until kids stop going the college route."

That's also how McCullough sees it: "Ultimately, until we address the fact that coaches are signing multimillion dollar contracts to control a largely Black labor force while that same labor force is denied adequate compensation, prohibited from unionizing, and literally killed from a lack of safety guarantees, plantation dynamics are here to stay, regardless of how much an individual athlete can make from their NIL."

Organizations to Contact

The editors have compiled the following list of organizations concerned with the issues debated in this book. The descriptions are derived from materials provided by the organizations. All have publications or information available for interested readers. This list was compiled on the date of publication of the present volume; the information provided here may change. Be aware that many organizations take several weeks or longer to respond to inquiries, so allow as much time as possible.

The Atlantic Coast Conference (ACC)

4512 Weybridge Lane
Greensboro, NC 27407
(336) 854-8787
website: www.theacc.com

The Atlantic Coast Conference is one of the Power Five conferences in collegiate sports. Students at ACC colleges compete in a wide range of sports, from field hockey to volleyball. The ACC was formed in 1953 with just seven schools. Today, the ACC includes Boston College, Clemson, Duke, Georgia Institute of Technology, Florida State, North Carolina State, Syracuse, Louisville, Miami, North Carolina, the University of Notre Dame, the University of Pittsburgh, the University of Virginia, Virginia Polytechnic Institute and State University, and Wake Forest University.

The Big Ten Conference

5440 Park Place
Rosemont, IL 60018
(847) 696-1010
website: www.bigten.org

Known as one of intercollegiate sports' most successful undertakings, the Big Ten is home to a lineage of legendary names and an ongoing tradition of developing strong leaders. Even in its infancy, the conference established itself as the preeminent collection of institutions in the nation, where the pursuit of academic excellence prevailed as the definitive goal. Big Ten schools include Illinois, Indiana, Iowa, Maryland, Michigan, Michigan State, Minnesota, Nebraska, Northwestern, Ohio State, Penn State, Purdue, Rutgers, and Wisconsin.

The Big 12 Conference

400 E John Carpenter Freeway
Irving, TX 75062
(469) 524-1000
website: www.big12sports.com

The Big 12 remains as the only autonomous conference to determine its champions in all sports directly on the field of play with a full round-robin schedule. The Big 12 has been at the forefront in college athletics reform, specifically with student-athlete welfare issues to include cost of attendance, student-athlete time demands, and strengthening its policy for concussion diagnosis and management.

Center for the Study of Sport in Society

101 Belvidere Street
Boston, MA 02115
(617) 373-4025
website: www.northeastern.edu/sportinsociety

Sport in Society educates and supports emerging leaders and organizations in sports. It provides the awareness, knowledge, and skills needed to implement innovative and impactful solutions for social change. Areas of focus include leadership, healthy development, diversity and inclusion, violence prevention, community building, community service, and civic engagement.

National Alliance of African American Athletes

PO Box 60743
Harrisburg, PA 17106-0743
(717) 312-8162
email: info@naaaa.com
website: www.naaaa.com

Established in 1989, the vision of the Alliance is to be the preeminent organization helping youth achieve academic excellence and reach their highest potential. The mission of the Alliance is to uplift and mentor youth, focusing on African American males, through programs that prepare students for college. The Alliance seeks to leverage athletes as catalysts to inspire leadership, while recognizing and rewarding academic, athletic, and community excellence.

The National College Players Association

PO Box 6917
Norco, CA 92860
(951) 898-0985
website: www.ncpanow.org

The National College Players Association was formed to protect college players in cases where the NCAA will not. Its goals include establishing mandatory health and safety standards, preventing players from paying sports-related medical expenses, increasing graduation rates, protecting educational opportunities and scholarships for college athletes in good standing, prohibiting universities from using a permanent injury suffered during athletics as a reason to reduce/eliminate a scholarship, and more.

The National Collegiate Athletic Association (NCAA)

700 W Washington Street
Indianapolis, IN 46204
(317) 917-6222
website: www.ncaa.org

The National Collegiate Athletic Association is a member-led organization dedicated to the well-being and lifelong success of college athletes. It is the umbrella association for college sports. NCAA schools award nearly $3.5 billion in athletic scholarships every year and provide vast support to help student-athletes graduate at a rate higher than their general student peers. The website's searchable database includes numerous articles on NIL, labor issues, and more.

The Pac-12 Conference

360 3rd Street
3rd Floor
San Francisco, CA 94107
(415) 580-4200
website: www.pac-12.com

The Pac-12 Conference is dedicated to developing the next generation of leaders by championing excellence in academics, athletics, and the well-being of its student-athletes. Beyond the courts and fields, the Pac-12's accomplishments extend into the classrooms across twelve campuses and outside its traditional geographic footprint into new corners around the world.

The Southeastern Conference (SEC)

2201 Richard Arrington Jr. Boulevard North
Birmingham, AL 35203
(205) 949-8960
email: secu@sec.org
website: www.secsports.com

The Southeastern Conference is a leader on the national landscape for intercollegiate athletics in the 21st century. Throughout its 82-year history, the SEC has provided leadership on the vital issues facing intercollegiate competition. Alabama, Auburn, Florida, Georgia, Kentucky, LSU, Mississippi, Mississippi State, Tennessee, and Vanderbilt have been in the SEC since its formation in 1933.

The league has expanded twice, adding Arkansas and South Carolina in 1991, then Missouri and Texas A&M in 2012.

Women's Sports Foundation (WSF)

247 West 30th Street
5th Floor
New York, NY 10001
(800) 227-3988
email: info@WomensSportsFoundation.org
website: www.womenssportsfoundation.org

The Women's Sports Foundation is dedicated to advancing the lives of girls and women through sports and physical activity. It supports the enforcement of Title IX of the Educational Amendments of 1972 and helps to educate the public through dissemination of facts, statistics, and background data on women in sports.

Bibliography

Books

Roger I. Abrams. *Sports Justice: The Law & the Business of Sports*. Boston, MA: Northeastern University Press, 2010.

John C. Barnes. *Same Players, Different Game: An Examination of the Commercial College Athletics Industry*. Albuquerque, NM: University of New Mexico Press, 2020.

Dana D. Brooks and Ronald C. Althouse. *Diversity and Social Justice in College Sports: Sport Management and the Student Athlete*. Morgantown, WV: Fitness Information Technology, 2007.

Gilbert M. Gaul. *Billion-Dollar Ball: A Journey Through the Big-Money Culture of College Football*. New York, NY: Penguin, 2016.

Cody T. Havard. *College Without Sport? Evaluating the Impact of Covid-19 on College Athletics and Lessons Learned*. Newbury Park, CA: SAGE Publications, 2021.

Kirsten Hextrum. *Special Admission: How College Sports Recruitment Favors White, Suburban Athletes*. New Brunswick, NJ: Rutgers University Press, 2021.

Joshua Hunt. *The Nike Effect: One Company's War on Higher Education, Organized Labor, and Clean Competition*. Brooklyn, NY: Melville House, 2020.

Frank P. Jozsa. *College Sports Inc: How Commercialism Influences Intercollegiate Athletics*. New York, NY: Springer, 2013.

Josh Luchs and James Dale. *Illegal Procedure: A Sports Agent Comes Clean on the Dirty Business of College Football*. New York, NY: Bloomsbury USA, 2013.

Joseph Nocera and Ben Strauss. *Indentured: The Battle to End the Exploitation of College Athletes.* New York, NY: Portfolio/Penguin, 2018.

Gary Alan Sailes. *Sports in Higher Education: Issues and Controversies in College Athletics.* San Diego, CA: Cognella, 2018.

Rick Telander, Rick Reilly, and Murray A. Sperber. *The College Football Problem: How Money and Power Corrupted the Game and How We Can Fix That.* New York, NY: Sports Publishing, 2020.

Gail Terp. *The Debate About Paying College Athletes.* Lake Elmo, MN: Focus Readers, 2018.

Andrew S. Zimbalist. *Whither College Sports: Amateurism, Athlete Safety, and Academic Integrity.* New Brunswick, NJ: Rutgers University Press, 2021.

Periodicals and Internet Sources

AB Staff. "The Highest Paid Public Employee in 39 States Is a Coach," *Athletic Business*, June 2018. https://www.athleticbusiness.com/operations/programming/news/15154661/the-highest-paid-public-employee-in-39-states-is-a-coach.

AB Staff, "Opinion: NCAA Business Model Is Broken," *Athletic Business*, March 1, 2018. www.athleticbusiness.com.

Chris Arkenberg, Lee Teller, and Michael Brodsky, "College Sports Opens the Door for Player Compensation," Deloitte, December 4, 2020. https://www2.deloitte.com.

Alan Blinder, "Big Contracts, Big Buyouts, Big Pressure: College Football Coaches Hit the Jackpot," *New York Times*, December 4, 2021. https://www.nytimes

.com/2021/12/04/sports/ncaafootball/college-football-coaching-changes.html.

Alan Blinder, "College Athletes Cash In as Generations of Rules Fade Under Pressure," *New York Times*, July 1, 2021. https://www.nytimes.com/2021/07/01/sports/ncaafootball/ncaa-college-athletes-endorsements.html.

Alan Blinder, "NCAA Misses Target to Approve Rules to Let Players Profit Off Their Fame," *New York Times*, September 29, 2021. https://www.nytimes.com/2021/06/23/sports/ncaafootball/ncaa-name-image-likeness-athletes-endorsements.html.

Andrew Brandt, "Business of Football: The Supreme Court Sends a Message to the NCAA," *Sports Illustrated*, June 29, 2021. https://www.si.com/nfl/2021/06/29/business-of-football-supreme-court-unanimous-ruling.

Liz Clarke, "State-by-State Rating System Gives College Recruits Road Map to Evaluate NIL Laws," *Washington Post*, October 21, 2021. https://www.washingtonpost.com/sports/2021/10/21/name-image-likeness-laws-state-rankings/.

Tom Dart, "The Case for Big-Time College Sports Helping Academics Remains Weak," *The Guardian*, September 28, 2021. https://www.theguardian.com/sport/2021/sep/28/the-case-for-big-time-college-sports-helping-academics-remains-weak.

Kristi Dosh, "Gatorade's First NIL Deal Is With Paige Bueckers," BCS: Business of College Sports, November 29, 2021. https://businessofcollegesports.com/name-image-likeness/gatorades-first-nil-deal-is-with-paige-bueckers/.

Mark J. Drozdowski, "Should College Athletes Be Paid?" Best Colleges, September 7, 2021. https://www.bestcolleges

.com/news/analysis/2021/09/07/should-college-athletes-be-paid/.

Jeff Faraudo, "Once Again, College Football Coaching Salaries Are Hard to Wrap Your Head Around," FanNation, October 15, 2021. https://www.si.com/college/cal/news/2021-coaching-salaries.

Sean Gregory, "As College Athletes Finally Start Cashing In, Entrepreneurs Big and Small Also Look to Score," *Time*, September 10, 2021. https://time.com/6094842/college-sports-nil-operndorse/.

Charles Lane, "Opinion: Can College Sports Survive Contact with the Truth?" *Washington Post*, June 22, 2021. https://www.washingtonpost.com/opinions/2021/06/22/can-college-sports-survive-ncaa-case/.

Dan Murphy, "Let's Make a Deal: NCAA Athletes Cashing In on Name, Image and Likeness," ESPN, July 1, 2021. https://www.espn.com/college-sports/story/_/id/31738893/ncaa-athletes-cashing-name-image-likeness.

Joe Nocera, "The Difference Between an Unpaid and a Paid Student-Athlete? Not Much," *New York Times*, October 4, 2021. https://www.nytimes.com/2021/10/23/business/college-endorsement-deals.html.

Kennington Lloyd Smith III, "How Important Will College Brand Value Be to Athletes in Name, Image and Likeness Era?" *USA Today*, July 2, 2021. https://www.usatoday.com/story/sports/college/2021/07/02/how-important-college-brand-value-athletes-name-image-likeness-era/5357047001/.

Index